Dogshit

Philip H. Bonello, Ph.D.

Library of Congress Control Number: 2012919260

ISBN-13: 978-0615540238
ISBN-10: 0615540236

Lake Shore Drive Press

For Julie, Philip, Peter, Mom, and Dad.
Thanks for your endless love and support…

"For God doth know that in the day ye eat thereof, then your eyes shall be opened, and ye shall be as gods, knowing good and evil." –Genesis 3:5

Author's Note

The United States Government is consumed by fear and with controlling two things which, coincidentally or not, each show themselves in the shape of a mushroom.

—PHB

"Evolution is very slow. It took a million years for man to figure out how to sharpen one side of a stone. It took man another million years to figure out how to sharpen the other side.

—Ray Kurzweil

Randy, wherever you are…

Foreword

This story began decades ago, many. A college acquaintance living in a storefront on Sheridan Road in Chicago's Rogers Park area had a few friends over. I was the brother to one of those friends. I was a doctoral student and these guys were college kids. I asked the host, "So, what's your life goal?" As if I had an answer for my own at the time. He responded with a goal, a *thought* that was so whacky that it stuck with me for decades. I mused that if he actually pursued it and succeeded, things here would indeed be different, really, really different. This *thought* became the load bearing pillar of this story and the choice of terms and language integral to the plot and title. He had said, "I want to grow a strain of psilocybin that grows on dogshit."

Years passed. There was never a story or a plot, characters or location, or even the idea of writing a book about it. This thought would periodically surface and then quickly become overrun by life's daily needs – love and support of family, hard work, career progress, the usual stuff.

Over time, and with the introduction of contemporary stories, contemporary characters and new technologies, a Vader vs. Yoda tale began to take form. The timeless struggle between Good against Evil.

It was a heavy weight bout: Hegel vs. Buddha and which path would lead to a better world. Not a new discussion, but now freshly nuanced and re-dimentionalized as I pondered my friend's stated life goal.

War and conflict are unquestionably powerful catalysts in propelling technology and advancing the human race, or so we think. The end goal is somehow to create and manage a better world. So far, this doesn't seem to working out so well.

So the question becomes, is there a less muscular, less bellicose alternative? Is there an intellectually aggressive *mechanism* to achieve the same through a diametrically opposite approach? And there the idea sat.

Then came the uber-scam of my lifetime, secret WMD's; Weapons of Mass Destruction cleverly hidden in Iraq by the United States' new arch nemesis. Never had more obvious bullshit been so easily passed along as fact to so many people – even thinking people. Sadly lives and resources were heavily committed to a pointless exercise. Pointless except for those who were in the war profiteering business–those in the business of thought and opinion management.

My antagonists had popped up like mushrooms after a light rain.

Then came The Great Recession and along with it, lots of time on my hands. My business had been sucked into the great cesspool of money management gone wild. I was now in the so-called good company of 158-year-old Lehman Brothers and 94-year-old Merrill Lynch, Washington Mutual, and thousands of others with names unknown to most. With finger to keyboard, this tale took shape, and along with it a newfound knowledge and respect for earth's most important and potent biological partner–fungi.

PART ONE

Chapter One

April 2011, in the outskirts of Palo Alto, California. It was 2:45 a.m. and Earp was still awake. Wide-awake. He'd been drinking, taking drugs, arguing with his wife, and petting his dogs.

He was sitting in his living room listening to Peruvian folk music, astounded for the thousandth time by the remarkably beautiful harmonies of Los Morochuucos de Peru and their lovely delivery in three-quarter time. His living room had a rough stone fireplace and small pieces of South American art here and there—gods, fertility figures—primitive, fierce, beautiful. There were photos of remote mountains with work-worn men and their mud-crusted Land Rovers. There were family photos and kindergarten art from grandchildren. It was a cozy little place, but there was palpable tension.

Earp was now too pissed off to sleep, so he poured another tall bourbon and walked downstairs to his office to check his e-mail. Francis Wyatt Earp, Jr., DVM, PhD was a distinguished-looking 68-year-old academic with flowing white hair and an oversized handlebar moustache and goatee. Earp was a veterinarian turned research botanist with a specialty in mycology. He was also a taxonomist extraordinaire. It was a true passion for him to find new plants or fungi and classify them. Earp had a specific interest in the fungi family. They were an odd life form. Although they were loosely classified under the umbrella of botanical life, morphologically, they were more similar to humans than to plants. Earp found their presence, their variations, their resilience, and their methods of reproduction intellectually attractive, biologically compelling in their reproductive and survival methods, and generally vexing in so many ways.

A veterinarian and botanist by education, he was trained to ask questions and search for answers. Earp was an inveterate reader and a sponge for knowledge. He looked at one of his recent stacks and scanned the titles—*The History of Salt, Hal's Legacy, South, Under the Volcano, The Magic Mountain, Medium Raw*, and *The Classic Cuisine of the Andes*—the reading list of an aggressive and acquisitive mind. Earp opened his daily journal and made several notes: Lichen as digesters for low grade plutonium? Speed of thought versus speed of light? Look for new coffee bean supplier, try adding brown sugar to water to extend fragrance of cut flowers? Revisit Everly Brothers.

Earp's current little neck of the intellectual woods was classifying plants and mushrooms. Plants old, new, and those yet to be discovered. After a few too many cocktails, Earp would often ramble with a slur to his friends, "*When the fucking shit hits the fan and they blow up the fucking world or create some other kind of global shitstorm of a disaster and everything goes to Hell, they'll be fuckin' lookin' for me! I'll be one of the few guys on the goddamn planet who will be able to figure out which shit we can eat and which shit will kill you. The field of taxonomy, the most fundamental part of information understanding and management, is fucking dead. No money, few students; we're fucked if we can't tell what shit is. Fucked, just fucked.*"

This was an important part of Earp's Worldview. He was also an awful and angry drunk.

Earp periodically displayed a near Buddhist-like awareness and concern for other people, but even with this other-oriented perspective, he was always just short of being moderately pissed off. Pissed off at whatever got him going, and it didn't take much to get him going. Even with these conflicting attitudes, or perhaps because of them, his mind was always racing with questions. He could never quite shut it off. His mind was like an engine that couldn't be killed. Thoughts woke him up in the middle of the night.

Sometimes his wife would find him asleep at his desk with the computer screen dimmed from insufficient use after he had been deep in a project for up to thirty hours without interruption. He could easily lose himself in thought or activity, only to be jolted back to temporal reality with a pat on the shoulders or a loud noise. He'd then curse in his head or aloud, "Jesus Christ, you mean it's Tuesday? What happened to Monday?"

Earp acknowledged to himself that his intellectual process was a blessing and curse and that there was nothing he could do about it. He likened it to a fireworks display, with thoughts and emotions exploding constantly. Sometimes they formed gestalts. Sometimes they were irritating in their apparent randomness. When he looked at his framed academic degrees and letters of recognition, he mused that it was a miracle he was able to actually accomplish anything, actually complete anything, due to his tireless and highly distractible nature.

Now Earp was in his basement, sitting at his cluttered desk and scrolling through e-mails and news feeds on his large Mac screen. He either deleted or skipped most of the stuff until he saw the e-mail from Sally. The subject was "new species, I think, maybe?!" Earp's first thought was, "*That woman doesn't have shit for brains. If her brain worked as well as her ass, there would be world peace."*

Sally was Earp's teaching assistant for mycology doctoral students and also for the school's undergrads. Sally was smart enough; Earp was just thinking like an asshole and was half in the tank. Sally was an unusual person. She was a brunette, about 5'6", very attractive, loved to have sex, and disliked alcohol and people who drank it, particularly to excess. Consequently, she was very discerning about her sexual partners and had the most unique filter for selecting them. Her favorite city was Jerusalem. She was a Jew, but didn't use her ethnicity or faith as her first calling card. She simply felt at home there. The history, the territorialism, the falafels, the will to survive, the bells, the diversity; there was no other place like it on earth.

Earp opened the e-mail and read the note. "Dr. Earp, Please take a look at the attached spectrograph and read my notes. Some of the molecular groups appear in such high concentrations that they significantly exceed default parameters and distort the decision branches. I am not sure how to classify this. Let's talk tomorrow. S."

It was time stamped six minutes ago at 2:59 a.m.

Earp opened the two files. The spectrography data folder was titled "Fungal Sample March 11, 2011, Source Unknown." Earp read the elements of the X-axis. There were 16. Then, he read the names of the two Y-axes. The left Y-axis was Equivalent Parts per Million. The right Y-axis was an element's Proportionate Contribution to the sample. After a quick look, Earp had three quick thoughts, *1) Sally really doesn't understand the software or there is a software error, 2) Sally is at least as stoned as I am, or 3) Sally may have unwittingly stumbled onto something.*

Earp quickly deconstructed the graph into two new ones, each with only one Y-axis. Then he examined the Y-scale parameters to more accurately reflect the relevance of the elements that occurred in very high or very low concentrations. Earp zero-based and range-based the scales so he could get a better understanding of the data's appearance. He popped open the Excel® spreadsheet to examine the raw data. It was here that Earp concluded that Sally had probably fucked things up. Some of these figures were way out of range. They didn't make sense, but they were unusual enough that Sally couldn't have missed them. This was perplexing. He thought, *Fuck it, she just sent me this thing, I'll call her. Too bad if it's 3:12 in the morning,* according to his 1968 Rolex Submariner wristwatch.

"Sally, hands up! Earp here. What is this stuff you just sent me and why are you writing about it at three in the morning? Everything okay?" Even though Earp drank a lot, even under the influence he could still think and reason fairly well. Earp would sometimes refer to himself as "a professional dipsomaniac." In his private, honest moments, he'd reflect that, call himself whatever he chose, it was still pronounced "alcoholic." But he avoided those moments assiduously.

"Thanks, Professor," Sally said. "Everything is fine. You really *do* care about people. You were just born ornery and learned to drink yourself into being even worse. And, sure, it's fine if you wake me up at 3:10 in the morning."

"Whatever, Sally…so, so sorry to have awakened you…and it's 3:12, by the way. Reset your watch. What is this stuff you just sent over, and where did it come from?" Earp barked a bit too loudly.

"I got it from a friend from college," Sally replied. "He said he bought some from a drug dealer and wanted to make sure they were safe before he ate them. He thinks it's ethneogenic and was told it was a powerful hallucinogen. He's another would-have-been botanist, but never pursued the field. We were close for a few years and then broke it off. But we've kept in touch periodically over the years. Now he's a struggling musician and walks dogs for a living."

"Sounds like an impressive young man," Earp snorted. "Do you have any more of the sample so that we can perform some additional tests?"

Sally said, "Well yeah, I have like ten grams."

"*Like*, where is it?" Earp mimicked her.

"It's in the refrigerator in Lab 714," Sally replied.

Earp said "Okay. Good. Let's talk tomorrow. Goodnight."

"Goodnight," said Sally.

Earp thought, *Ethneogenic? I'll say, if these concentrations are close to being accurate, we have God herself locked up in the refrigerator.*

This was the both the most toxic and the most distorted concentration of these specific psychotropic elements Earp had ever seen. And he had seen them all and tried most of them, or so he thought. This was new and had the potential to wreak real havoc.

It was also something that clearly had not occurred in nature all by itself. The substance had the fingerprints of human intellect all over it. The organic chemical engineers could be the Russian Mafia, part of a wealthy drug cartel looking for some new designer drug, or the CIA, but this was not a just a freak of nature. Earp was extraordinarily intrigued and, being honest with himself, a little frightened. There was a story behind this and it probably was not a good one. It might also prove to be a dangerous one. Whatever it was he would find out soon enough. Right now, his mind was on fire.

Earp immediately turned on his 1940 vintage Pavoni espresso machine so that he could get a quick cup of coffee after his shower and shave. He liked the old espresso machine because of its Art Deco elegance, efficient functionality, chrome finish, and that a cup of espresso needed to be pressed by hand. He felt as if he'd earned his coffee because making it actually required some physical force.

Earp always looked sharp and played the part of the erudite academician and research scientist. He thought tonight might be the beginning of something special and decided to dress for the occasion, so he selected a white, all cotton, long-sleeved guayabera.

He was a smooth operator and politically astute. He had an acerbic wit, an encyclopedic knowledge of several scientific fields and loved to display his vast knowledge. The word pedantic was created for him. When Earp wanted to be charming, he was Clintonesque. You could feel his presence and energy when he entered the room. He projected an affable aloofness, like someone floating through and over the room of people, with a hint of a smile that he was the only one who really got the joke. But when he focused on you, you believed you'd found your new best friend. You'd never know that as soon as he'd turned away, you were out of his mind. He had traveled the world and had stories of adventure and near-death that were vivid enough to enthrall even the most uninterested snobs.

Earp could also talk money out of anyone. The "Institution," as Earp referred to it, both hated and loved him. He operated with a free rein. One of his little money-gathering tricks was selling the right to name newly discovered plants. Earp would offer this right to financial donors. In other words, an egomaniacal donor could name a plant or species after himself—or his cat for that matter. Earp found the whole concept and process extremely distasteful and was chronically disgusted with himself for prostituting his ethics and scientific interests for money. For $50,000, however, one of his newly discovered plants would forever carry the name of its millionaire benefactor. If Earp found a new species, he'd charge more.

Once a dim-witted potential donor asked in a very serious and scholarly sounding voice,

"But Dr. Earp, how do you really—I mean, *really*—know the plant is truly new and not recorded somewhere else by someone else?"

He responded politely, swallowing his reflexive arrogance and distain, and instead laying a reassuring hand on the woman's shoulder. He knew better than to let his distaste distract him from a sizeable check. "I've been crawling around on the ground studying plants and mushrooms for 43 years. I can assure you that if I personally have not seen it before, it did not exist."

Earp drove his 1963 mint condition sea foam green Volvo 444 down the winding road from his home to the highway. It was an old, odd, but distinguished car. He had found it in Peru years ago and managed to slip it into the states through Mexico.

In fourteen minutes, he was on campus. Earp pulled into his office parking lot. It was about four a.m., dark and quiet. He locked his car with a hand key and walked alone toward his office with his mind racing. What the fuck was this stuff and *who* was behind it?

Although he was exited about the sample he was about to see, he felt oddly and uncharacteristically ill at ease. He looked around to see if there was someone was watching him. He got some goose bumps, but quickly shook them off.

Chapter Two

About six months earlier in the outskirts of Palo Alto, California "Heidi!" Julie yelled. "If you eat one more thing from this counter, we're going to have you for dinner tonight! How many times do I have to tell you stay off this counter!" Julie had bought those morels, shipped all the way from Pennsylvania, for a special sauce. "You have to be the only dog on the planet that eats vegetables, not to mention mushrooms."

The brown English setter was completely unfazed by the threat and continued to paw its way around the counter of her newly remodeled kitchen. Julie quickly put some dog food in a bowl and sprinkled some shredded cheese on it to encourage Heidi to try the new food she had purchased. This new food was a special organic blend that contained rice hulls. The hulls were added to bulk up the food's fiber content.

Julie loved to study and had researched this food additive. She was a bit surprised and somewhat pleased to learn that rice hulls are used in a wide variety of industrial applications, from specialized fertilizer to pet food. The hull is the hard, outermost shell that protects the rice that most people are familiar with as a food product. The hard hull or husk must be separated from the edible part of the rice to produce food. In ancient times, and today in underdeveloped countries, tossing the dried rice in the air took care of this separation, letting the wind blow away the hull. The edible rice, being heavier, fell back in the basket.

Julie was glad to learn that the non-edible portion of the plant had found a useful purpose. She fervently believed that everything on earth had a purpose and that we were just beginning to understand the uses in the bounty of all things natural. She would tell her staff and family, "God, being the really smart woman she is, didn't waste any time creating things of no value. God wasted nothing. Ecological competition and the evolutionary dynamics of survival take care of the weaklings."

Julie had done some work with these hulls about fifteen years before, so she was familiar with their use as a mesoporus molecular sieve and as a chemical catalyst. They worked in the same fashion as a coffee filter, but at the molecular level. Hulls were also used as support systems for drug delivery and as absorbents in water treatment. Extremely versatile, they occur in great abundance and at financial and environmental cost.

Julie was amused that these relatively sophisticated cast offs were now in her dog's food. They were being added to pet food because of their low cost and their ability to improve the financial yield per pound. Because of their high fiber count, the hulls aided digestion, peristalsis and, as with many high fiber food stuffs, they passed through the digestive tract and remained more or less in tact in the stool. They were good for Heidi's digestion – lots of good fiber.. Julie also discovered they were also becoming increasingly popular as additives to fertilizer. The hull-enhanced fertilizer was uniquely hospitable to certain types of food products, particularly those in the fungus family.

For a dog, Heidi had a wonderful personality. Everyone commented on it. Even their dog walker, Rob, said that of all the dogs he has known, Heidi was one of the most pleasant to be around. When Rob said this to Julie she thought, *I'll bet he tells that to all the dog owners*. But, Heidi was a very nice dog and she did have an unusually broad interest in foodstuffs. She ate fruit and raw vegetables among other foods that most dogs didn't care for.

Their remodeled kitchen was a great aesthetic and functional remodeling achievement for Julie. She'd researched everything that went into it. She knew how porous all of the countertop materials were, how much maintenance each one required, and their useful lives—she could drive people crazy with her thoroughness and her ability to quickly get up to speed on just about any topic.

She ultimately decided upon one of those trendy, state-of-the-art tinted and custom molded concrete jobs found in the nicest of kitchens these days, a special complement to complete the renovation she had done to their house last year. *Glad to have that nasty rehab business behind the family,* she thought. Julie was busy on a salami sandwich for 9-year-old Peter, a turkey sandwich for 12-year-old Philip, juggling a couple bowls of cereal and some eggs for breakfast, and thinking through a preparation for a faux beef Wellington with the morel sauce, if Heidi left any of them for her.

Julie had purchased one of those *Grow 'Ur Own Exotic Mushroom* microenvironments that allowed her to have a recurring supply of fresh shitake, oyster, morel, and a few other useful fungi for her cooking needs. It had made sauce- and omelet-making easier and a lot less expensive. Nothing like the fragrance of fresh mushrooms to jazz up just about any dish. The mushrooms just kept on producing once the environment was stabilized. It was the perfect confluence of nerdy science and haute cuisine. Julie loved the thing. Then a week or so ago, Heidi knocked it off the counter. When she did, the plastic housing broke apart. Heidi not only ate the mushrooms, but also ate most of the dirt and growing medium. *What a weird fucking dog*, Julie thought.

Julie finished her breakfast- and lunch-making duties and then rushed to her bedroom to get dressed for this oh-so-secret meeting. *I'll doll myself up a bit*, she thought. *A little distraction might come in handy.* She looked in the mirror and added a little mascara, something she normally didn't use. She brushed her sleek red hair, and twisted it into a simple bun. She used a pair of chopstick-like pins to hold it in place. *Don't you ever die!* she told herself. She knew that she, 43 or not, was still a beautiful woman and, in the world of science and venture capital, good looks go a long way.

Her old genius colleague, John, came to mind. For as long as Julie could remember, when she thought about somebody, a former college pal, there would be a similar thought by the other party. It had happened so many times in her life. She'd be wondering about a former college pal and minutes later the phone would ring. It was eerie at first, but she concluded the wavelengths were simply in the air and that somehow she had developed better than average antennae.

Back to today's reality! she said to herself. The day was scrolling fast—call it par for a Monday morning—but Julie couldn't take her mind off the meeting that was scheduled for 10:30 at HGMP. This meeting was an unusually secretive one. Only Julie, Paulo, the company's president, and Carl, the second in command and Julie's longtime pal, were attending. Something important was up.

Julie was lucky to be working for Human Genome Mapping Projects, Inc., not just because the company itself was cool. It had a wonderful work climate. As she got dressed, she recalled her first visit to the campus and how excited she'd been that day.

People were fired-up, engaged in their projects, talking enthusiastically about their work. The cafeteria felt like an art gallery, with photos of musicians including Hendrix, Duke Ellington, and a painting of Bach, gazing down from the walls. There was an original oil painting by Donald Van Vliet, also known as Captain Beefheart. There was a large drawing of the Father of Science above the main entrance. The first time Julie saw it and every time since, she imagined Archimedes running naked through the streets after discovering Pi. Julie loved the eclectic intellectualism and that management made it part of the corporate culture to keep the employees aware of the company's initiatives. There was a short weekly meeting dedicated to updates and a Q&A. She typically had low regard for human resources bureaucrats; but these HR folks knew their stuff. Each year they published a book and anybody could write anything about anyone or any topic. People played nice with each other.

HGMP's niche in genomics addressed the challenge of mapping genes to correlate those genes and their characteristics to related diseases or other organically-based commercial needs. If they got lucky, the groundwork was then laid for possible cures. They were closely tied into research institutions like Chicago's Field Museum, the Pritzker Foundation, the Centers For Disease Control, NASA, the National Cancer Institute, the National Institutes of Health, the Howard Hughes Foundation, and many other outstanding research organizations.

Building predictive models on how the molecular structures and functions of DNA, RNA, and proteins worked—and their sequences of operation—were primary tasks of HGMP. Another major set of tasks was taxonomically building clusters of genes into functional groups. Perhaps most significant, however,

HGMP had an entire department devoted to "cleaning up" data sets and filling in missing links or values. This research department was called JPR, named after the book and movie *Jurassic Park*, which had introduced this scientific concept to the general public. The Jurassic Park Research team even had their own polo shirts with little raptorsaurus logos embroidered on them with the slogan "If we fill 'em, you can grow 'em" embroidered on them. It was admittedly hokey, but these were some uber-nerdy people.

The knee of the technology curve was just starting to take off for man. The slow slog through the past few thousand years was now starting to get truly interesting. Big change was occurring and at an increasingly faster rate each day. Their field was a prime example. Twenty-five years ago, it didn't even exist. It now had the potential to change the world. Biotechnology was the next big thing, and they were all over it.

Chapter Three

The fictional case for building dinosaurs had been the best public relations boost anybody could have imagined for HGMP. Everyone wanted to get in on the action, from old ladies hoping to recreate a deceased cat, to meat producers looking to recreate the mammoth, to the military scheming to breed highly aggressive dinosaurs to use as weapons. One wacky military proposal involved crossbreeding the T. rex with a Doberman Pinscher. The hybrid creature would thereby become obedient and highly trainable. The proposal's author had digitally restaged the battle of Normandy, but instead of men jumping from boats into the water, it changed the players and had many hundreds of obedient T. rex dinosaurs leaping from large ships and racing into enemy fire. There were some serious wack jobs working in the military-industrial complex these days. Eisenhower was right when he issued his forewarning to be aware and concerned about the emerging military-industrial complex.

In *Jurassic Park*, fictional scientists had an idea about where to find the missing piece of genetic code to flesh-out a complete DNA string. The story made the process seem logical and straightforward. In fact, it was mostly guesswork, but nonetheless, it was really interesting stuff.

HGMP's data center was a sight to behold. Although a lot of computing was moving into the cloud, due to HGMP's top-secret work and the financial and military value of many of their contracts, they maintained their own facilities—two of them. They were mirror images of each other and they balanced their processing between the two facilities. They remained current in each location all the time with no more than a 15-minute delay on data integrity between the sites. The data centers were in different locations and connected through elaborate telecommunications networks. The networks were not simply redundant, but also route-diverse. So, if a major telecommunications backbone became disrupted because of an attack or natural disaster, the backup route would still allow work to continue and their data would be protected.

Entering the data center involved several levels of identification. The first was a retinal scan, which opened a passage chamber similar to a large revolving door in an airport. Once inside one of the revolving door's three sections, a voice match was required. Upon verification, the door would advance one third of its turn. Finally, a handprint match would advance the door to its final position for passage into the center. It was clearly overkill on security, but the government contract managers and their clients loved the extremity of their efforts. On a rare and exceptional case, a non-employee would be granted access to the data center itself. If a visit inside the data center didn't make them feel super-important, nothing did. The data center was vast, housing thousands of servers networked together to deliver breathtaking processing capabilities. They processed multiple batches of many terabytes of data on a daily basis.

The next hundred years would be nothing short of breath-taking in terms of scientific and medical advances. Diseases would be eliminated at the core, and among other areas in which HGMP was tinkering were intelligence and perception. Intelligence was being channeled and hyper-developed. They were enhancing certain parts of the brain's anatomy and physiology to produce superhuman analytical capabilities. They had created idiot savant-type chimps, for example, who were really good at geometric puzzle solving. They weren't good at much else, but they could piece together complex puzzles in record times.

They were developing hyper-perception and promoting the idea with irresistibly enticing imagery. For example, some women would be able to elect to have the sight of eagles. Some men would elect to have the same sense of smell as Julie's nutty English setter. The age of the real X-Men was not far away. Things that were once considered anatomical requirements or constrained by process or data capture limitations would be overcome with genetic engineering. Heightened perception, with the aid of implanted microprocessors and gene manipulation would begin to produce super-people and super-animals. After all, it was all about wavelength perception. Some biological creatures perceived some electromagnetic wavelengths much better than others. Fundamentally, it was a very simple paradigm. Now there were sufficiently powerful computers to assist in the process, and this computing power was quickly migrating closer and closer to the end user.

Their research also came with risks. The old advertising slogan, "*It's not nice to fool with Mother Nature*," was always on the researchers' minds. It was just a matter of time until there was going to be some kind of major fuckup.

Chapter Four

HGMP was nestled in a tasteful, but relatively nondescript building on the outskirts of Palo Alto. Its founder Paulo Verdoccia had come to Stanford from Italy to study biology. Paulo had made boatloads of money during the dotcom boom through his early investments in companies like Yahoo, Netscape, and eBay. Paulo used his winnings to help fund his own startup. Paulo thought like a biologist, so he had developed a keen appreciation for the phenomenon of explosive growth and the deadly consequences that frequently occur as a result. Some of the most promising companies Paulo had invested in were either already dead or had been gobbled up by a competitor.

Paulo's business acumen got him out of those investments at the just right time and made him a series of small fortunes in the process, establishing himself as an astute businessman and making some influential contacts in the process. With all of this, Paulo parlayed his small fortunes into a substantial fortune and could now throw around his considerable financial weight. Paulo was particularly well connected in Washington and enjoyed a large number of lucrative defense contracts. Conflict had been profitable historically, and his esoteric area of technology was no exception. That was one of the reasons Paulo had founded HGMP.

The employees and many of the townspeople affectionately referred to the company as HugMap. It had as its published and fully internalized corporate vision: "*To provide the map and keys to all biologically-based functions, to unlock the secrets to the essence of being, and to build longer, better, and more productive lives.*"

This sounded lofty, but the science and the tools were there to make some truly great leaps forward. As a consequence, the work culture at HugMap had a bit of a highbrow attitude. The employees believed that they were on the cusp of doing something really important. The HugMap people felt that they were a part of the next renaissance. They believed, and not without good reason, that they were on the brink of doing something fundamentally transformative for humankind. It was quite a feeling, and they were right. They thought the guys at Google were real smart and doing cool stuff, but it was just search, ads, communication, and energy use. Google had now become the Country's second largest user of electricity, so they were getting smart about how to use it efficiently and cost effectively. Big deal, but not so big.

Paulo, on the other hand, was regarded as a latter-day Leonardo, Michelangelo, and Galileo all rolled into one man. He had money, power, creativity, and scientific vision all under one hat. He was providing the environment, the culture, the money, and the spirit to do great things. Somebody had to lead. Somebody had to have vision, and by statistical definition, most of the rest had to follow. Paulo was at the front of the pack and he could see the end of the road, or at least convince everyone else he could. He was the Steve Jobs of bioinformatics and genomics.

HugMap had a mission, a vision, energy, ambition, and the resources to do pretty much whatever it wanted to do. So it did.

As a firm, one of its primary goals was to develop a better understanding of the origins of life. This was a complex subject that covered everything from panspermia to the chemical composition of the Earth's early atmosphere and how it could support primitive biological organisms. HugMap intended to change the world.

HugMap was well financed, well structured, and privately held. It had plenty of capital, bankers if necessary, and investor relationships. It held hundreds of active patents, many already revenue-producing. Some of the earth's brightest people were dedicated employees. It had the best computer processing technology money could buy, and if there was a need for more capacity or more IT guys in a pinch, CERN, Fermi Lab, Caltech, MIT, and Los Alamos were on Paulo's speed dial.

Even considering the breadth and depth of all its resources, the task HGMP had taken on was nothing short of daunting—to sequence and fine-map every identifiable part of human genetic code. After discovery, the scientists would classify each piece they found. After enough data in a particular area was captured and classified, they would develop predictive models in the hope of solving a specific problem, such as what, at the genetic level, causes acne or color blindness. They would then attempt to reverse-engineer desired outcomes. In the course of routine work, ideas would pop. In a way, it was like practicing music. In the routines of practicing scales, variations would arise. HGMP had a seemingly bottomless well of routines and as a consequence, new and creative hypotheses were introduced all the time. HGMP's primary focus was on the human body and there was sufficient work to keep many people busy for many, many decades.

The human body has one hundred million, million cells (100,000,000,000,000). Each cell has a complete set of the human genome or map of the human DNA. HugMap planned to visit every minuscule nook and cranny of the genome, and then map, taxonomically classify, document, and patent what was found, particularly those discoveries appearing to have the greatest commercial potential. But it was often impossible to tell which things had commercial potential and which things didn't. They were tinkering with some very esoteric materials and as Buckminster Fuller said, "many discoveries are nonspontaneously illuminating." In other words, the value or potential of a discovery isn't always obvious, or shit happens and sometimes you are not sure why.

HGMP had a simple process with highly complex component parts. A scientist would get an idea about a solution or a direction on a problem, that is, what kind of code would fill in the blank on a particular "fill problem." An example would be, "what were the genetic code attributes or sequences for polio or cancer or AIDS?" A section of DNA might be identified as being responsible for managing a particular disease or controlling the range of wavelengths the human ear could physiologically recognize and then cognitively process, but that might be all that was known. How to manipulate those variables and how to control disease or extend the perceptual wavelength range and the use of those perceptions was a completely different set of problems and challenges.

So, a data set, or range would be created, and then an array of high-speed processors could run for weeks, dropping in numbers from various data sets until all the values in the range had been used. Even after all this effort, the results usually didn't produce anything but goose eggs. Then, it was back to the drawing board for a new set of bright ideas.

It was often very frustrating work. When the ideas worked, however, it was like winning the Lotto. Raw exhilaration and occasionally life changing consequences were the result. Sometimes, there was hope for people who before the breakthrough had none. Those breakthroughs made up for all the hard work and frustration. There were real accomplishments. HGMP had developed cures for spino bifida and psoriasis and were very close to coming up with a solution for malaria. The Bill and Melinda Gates Foundation alone had provided a full decade's worth of funding for the malaria research, no strings attached.

Chapter Five

J uliet Bridgette Perthuis—everyone had called her Julie since she was eleven—was the complete package. She was six feet tall, with shoulder-length red hair and a thin athletic figure. She jogged in the California hills around their home a few times a week. She wore casual, expensive, conservative clothes and used relatively little makeup. She didn't need much. Now in her early forties, she was still a head turner. In her twenties, she was a conversation stopper. That was particularly true when Julie was at MIT, where nerds are not known for their good looks.

Julie always liked school and did well in her studies. Because she didn't have to work very hard in school, she had a lot of time to read, think, play sports, and socialize. She once bet the kids in her operations research class that she could outscore all of them on the final exam without opening the book until the night before the exam. She asked her professor for dispensation on the interim test and said she wanted to bet the farm on only the final. Her professor strongly advised against it, but let her do it anyway.

"It's your future and your money," Professor Thomas said. "Most students have a difficult time with my class under normal conditions. You may do as you wish, young lady, but don't come back looking for my sympathetic ear."

Julie's ambition had been magnified by the professor's demeaning use of "young lady." She received the highest grade in the class.

Due in part to her good looks, she had a great many doors opened to her that others didn't. College was an eye-opening experience for her, as it is for most young people. She had a few brilliant and inspirational teachers. She had a good dose of liberal politics. She had her first real relationship with a real man. She had a number of memorable drinking sessions and tried the requisite range of popular recreational drugs. That's what everyone did in those days. It was just part of college, even at MIT.

All of this was now just part of her distant college memories, except for those uniquely memorable experiences with psilocybin. There was something unique about the psilocybin experience. It had an otherworldly aspect. There was an antenna that became active. Those fungi added an element of clarity, or more accurately, removed a filter. They significantly increased the rate of information uptake and capture. They really made her think. They made her look at everything differently, more creatively, critically, and expansively. Those experiences helped her define her role in the world and her role in the universe; at least it seemed so at the time. They gave her a vibe and allowed her to believe she could sense others who had the same psychoactive or mind-expanding experiences as she'd had. As Huxley put it, others who had also walked "through the doors of perception."

Those conclusions were probably accurate, she subsequently decided, because all perception is the result of recognizing specific electromagnetic wavelengths. She now believed that the psilocybin had modified certain receptors. As far as Julie was concerned, those few experiences changed her views of the world for the better, and for the *forever*. They left an impression she never got over and she was better off for it. Mushrooms also intrigued Julie because their morphology was more similar to humans than to that of plants. It was just an odd fact. This fact coupled with their impact on cognition and perception made them a great curiosity for her when she was in school.

Julie didn't dwell on the subject. She had moved on to the real world long ago. She had a husband, two kids, two cars, a dog and a job. Every once in a while, however, as she was trying to go to sleep, she did wonder just what that stuff was all about. Julie operated under the assumption that everything on earth was here for a reason. Each thing had a purpose. So, what was psilocybin's purpose?

Chapter Six

It was a strange and highly polarized time in America. Politics had run amuck. Half the population, including people like Julie's husband, Clark, were nothing short of thrilled to have had a right-wing arm firmly controlling the political agenda. Their fundamentalist Christian backers had the oil-rich military industrial complex funding their conservative causes. Their methods were to create enemies and start fights. They started wars. They built lots of stuff with taxpayer dollars. The United States had become the world's largest supplier of weapons and war-support products. It was an unholy and immoral business. It did create a lot of jobs, but more to the point, it made a large number of influential people very, very wealthy.

In addition to war profiteering, these so-called conservatives were restoring their interpretation of good old-fashioned American values. Like them or not, these guys were very effective in getting things done and downright brilliant at managing the message. They were not doing the good things as Aristotle would have defined them, but they did get a lot of things done and had elaborate and well-distributed propaganda machines. They had their own television channel and positioned themselves as the only objective source of the truth. The news channel called itself Hound News and they were astoundingly, if not frighteningly effective. Half of Americans actually believed the stuff they spewed out each day. It was easy to steer the thinking of most Americans. The nation's population was increasingly poor and isolated from "full world" experiences. Eighty percent of Americans never left their home state. The political and financial market leaders had also consolidated the financial wealth of the nation into a very small percentage of the country's population. One half of one percent of the people controlled over half the country's money. The four hundred richest American families had more money than the entire bottom half of the US population combined. That is, four hundred families had more money than the combined net worth of 165,000,000 people. The only time in America's history when something similar had occurred was in 1929.

Clark thought "our administration," as he liked to refer to them, could do very little wrong. He and Julie had a very good marriage, many discussions about domestic policy, social policy, and foreign policy. They disagreed on most political topics. It was remarkable they were in love with each other considering their significant differences in areas of public policy and governance. They did share a belief in family, honesty, education, and putting their children first.

Julie would often say to Clark, "Listen, Honey Pie, people have been arguing over these same mostly bullshit issues for centuries. They will still be sorting themselves out long after you and I are dead and gone—maybe. For us, these largely pointless topics give us a never-ending opportunity to exercise our minds and still do our most important jobs—raise Philip and Peter."

Clark, being a red-blooded man at heart, would usually give in and exit the debate with something like, "Okay, sweetness, you win again. What do you say we smoke a joint and finish this debate in bed? The boys are sleeping. All of this talk about military might has made me really horny."

If there was one area where the Red states agreed with the Blue states, it was that they each liked to smoke green.

And, off they went. Julie believed, although she never mentioned her theory to Clark, that when he short-circuited their political discussions this way it was, in addition to his stated reasons, because he knew he didn't have an ethical leg to stand on and he was on the brink of losing the argument.

Chief among their differences was having the Justice Department and those of the former Attorney General, James Arkloft, define social and moral policy.

Arkloft was steely eyed and six foot four. Other than his height, Arkloft was an average-looking man. He wore conservative dark suits, white button-down shirts and usually striped ties with at least two of the red, white, and blue in their design. He was actually very ordinary in every way except for his views on politics, governance, and religion. In these areas, he was an outlier, even among those who shared his views. Although now out of office, he was still very much engaged in political action. He was closely aligned with the oil and gas industries and the large infrastructure-building companies that had giant government and military contracts.

Arkloft's Justice Department had been significantly expanded—both its staffing and general funding—under his direction. The department had implemented political action and spending initiatives in every meaningful judicial contest at every level in the country. They were building the judicial constituency for the next century. Arkloft was always on a private plane darting off to small towns across America promoting his agenda.

He was a sight to behold. Arkloft often gave his speeches in high school gyms. He would stand before a crowd of barely literate but enthusiastic listeners and preach to them, not with fire and brimstone, but with the dispassionate tone of a good teacher. You could also feel the energy of power and the power of the energy. White men in good shape, wearing good suits, stood at the far ends of the stage. Their peers and other members of the security detail stood at the entrances and exits. Each of them wore sunglasses and high-tech earbuds. They carefully watched the people and listened for orders or updates from an unknown command post, probably in the parking lot.

Parked outside this school were a half dozen black SUVs with tinted windows and three or four black vans. Inside the vans, IT personnel watched the crowd on LED monitors and iPads®. They remotely controlled cameras that had been mounted 50 miles away several weeks earlier. These cameras had lenses that were a foot in diameter and could be operated with the ease of a $149 Canon Powershot®. The cameras were all connected through groups of iPhones®.

The IT guys zoomed in on a few Vietnam War vets, a small group of longhaired students wearing Bob Marley T-shirts, a group of NRA promoters, and others. Every face was digitally captured and matched against images on various government databases and of course, Facebook. Adding to the drama of the well-crafted display of power was the loud throbbing whir of the helicopter blade as the chopper made its sweep of the school grounds and surrounding area.

After calling upon his supporters and admirers to join him in a short prayer, he'd begin to evangelize about God, America, and our preordained rights and obligations. He would wait for silence and then say in a soft but assured voice, "My fellow Americans, we are here together today not because of voting or polling or well-designed campaigns. Not because of our great party. We are here together because God, our one and only God, and our savior Jesus Christ, brought this day *to us*. This is our collective calling as God defined it in the great Constitution of the United States. We are a Nation under God. We are here not to celebrate the fact that America is, without dispute, the greatest country this world has ever seen, but rather we are here to put our minds, our souls, our family, and our faith toward the pursuit of a greater goal. We have been given the responsibility of spreading God's word to others. Others around the world who have yet to see God's grace and wisdom. We have been given the political will and the political power to change the world for the better. Today our way of life is threatened and this is due precisely to the absence of the fundamental Christian truths that we cherish and hold to be so very basic. These truths are our rights. Because of our enemies' misplaced faith in false Gods, members of foreign countries and even people on our own soil pursue evil and violence. It is you and I and millions of others who share a profound responsibility to take action, regardless of the means or methods, to see that throughout the world, our Lord's word is spread and that Jesus is the one and only son of the one and only God. Americans are God's chosen people. Please now, bow your heads and pray with me today."

Thus, the Attorney General of the United States helped re-shape political boundaries throughout the country.

Somehow, someway, *they were going to legislate thought*. It was part of their plan to legislate morality. They believed that the majority of people were not intellectually capable or qualified to even contribute to high-level thought on governance. Arkloft believed he and his associates were the philosopher kings of our day. They believed that they had been chosen to direct the people and to define the moral and ethical boundaries of the modern word. Not since the Inquisition had organized religion exercised so much influence on political and social policy.

Clark thought this was all just fine. After all, just a few years ago, the United States had a President boning a twenty-some-thing intern in the oval office. What kind of image was that for American youth and the world?

On his way up the ladder of power, Arkloft's conservative message resonated quickly with the population in his largely rural home state, and he capitalized on this sentiment to capture power and become the state's attorney general. When the evangelical right stole the White House with hanging chads, they wanted to ensure that their most important agenda items received all the attention they deserved. They plucked Arkloft out of the rural South and dropped him into Washington. Remarkably, he was even more controversial and polarizing than the rest of his administration, lionized by half the population and feared and detested by the other half.

Among his many professional responsibilities, Arkloft was also of counsel for Roune and Brute and for Bellihurton. He was a very close aide to Charles "Chick" Daney. Chick was the country's former vice president and had been the principal architect of the nation's foreign and domestic policies. Depending on your point of view, Charles Daney was either the world's savior who could thumb his nose at the law to further the cause of freedom, or Darth Vader incarnate. James and Chick were asshole buddies.

Arkloft ran a tight operation in his stewardship of the Justice Department. Fervent belief in God was the most important criterion for job acceptance and placement. Arkloft thought the only thing more offensive than an atheist was a believer who was a non-fundamentalist. There was a great irony that fundamentalist Muslim thinking fueled the terrorist activity in the Middle East and that America's fundamentalist Christians were fueling the New American Politics. It was the Crusades all over again. This time, however, the Arab world seemed to be really fighting back. They also had the opiate of technology working for them, oil. This discussion-rich subject received remarkably little media attention. Their money was clearly very well spent in owning their own media conglomerates. It was a page right out of the Joseph Goebbels' playbook.

For Arkloft, morality was the essential root of all behavior, and therefore, something that could and should be legislated. This notion spoke to the very essence of controlling consciousness and the quality and range of thought. A true conservative, by his definition, didn't think expansively. On the contrary, there was no need to expand one's range of thought. The more narrow the thought the more focused the population. In this regard, he disapproved of drinking, dancing, premarital sex, non-missionary sex, drugs, and anything that was not fundamentally pure and in keeping with his Christian views. He believed the law should be used as an unforgiving force of enforcement, vengeance or even revenge if necessary to move his view of God's message and his personal calling forward. There was no other way. This was the right thing to do and this was his chosen path. Arkloft routinely compared himself to Jesus and referred to his projects and campaign victories as "resurrections." He reflected on his occasional failures as "crucifixions."

He was driven by blind conviction. He was truly a dangerous man, made all the more dangerous because he had unlimited resources.

Chapter Seven

As soon as Julie got into her office she called her buddy Carl. "Morning, Carl," Julie said. "Any idea what's cooking at 10:30?"

Carl said, "Nope. This *is* a quiet one. It's almost like Paulo's spooked or something. I haven't seen him act like this since the bombing in Oklahoma City."

"That's odd," Julie said.

"What? Paulo's behavior or my comparison?" Carl asked.

"Both," Julie said. "It must have popped up out of the blue."

"Well I'll see you at ten thirty, and I can't wait," Carl said with a smile in his voice.

Julie opened her system and checked the newsfeed she had created for herself. She got updates on local high school sports, various highly technical subjects in her fields of interest, the latest from Wikileaks. She really admired the work this organization was doing, but she was also wary that her firm could be targeted and hacked. They had some really smart people ready to fall on their swords, if necessary.

Julie reviewed her calendar for this week and next, and for

the following month. She e-mailed her secretary to make a few changes in meeting times and to get a shower gift for one of her staff. She looked out her window at the immense granite sphere and wondered about the meeting she was about to attend. The sphere was great for pondering. It was twenty feet in diameter and had been sculpted on site, in its current position. She often thought, *Just about everything moves a little, but not that sphere.* She was comforted by its reliable presence.

She was usually privy to the inner workings of almost all of the company's projects. Most of these projects were highly classified and required high level government and military security clearance. Julie, her colleague, Carl, and Paulo each had TS clearance. Top Secret security clearance was not afforded to many in the private sector and was considered a significant achievement. Julie was able to read information and access files only available to top military officials, senior level CIA, and select members of the nation's three branches of government. As far as Julie knew, however, the only person who knew what was going on in this meeting was Paulo. They had an important potential new client from Texas. That was all Julie knew.

She took the elevator down two floors underground, and walked down the hall to room Zero. She always marveled at the extremes Paulo had taken to create this special conference room, what was known as a Faraday cage. She was both proud of its technical sophistication and creeped out by the need for it. Room Zero had two, one-inch thick steel panels with lead sandwiched between these two heavy metal sheets. This structure was behind the interior plaster wall. The room had no wireless access and any computer used in the room was routed through a dedicated server that only supported that room. There were no light fixtures per se in the room. The room was the light fixture. The walls and the ceiling were fully covered with Organic Light Emitting Diodes or OLEDs. The lighting was ample, easy on the eyes, diffuse, and battery powered. There had been a couple of "suits" that had swept the area to ensure there were no bugs. HGMP people swept the room every morning and evening. These Texans wanted their own independent sweep.

When the meeting began, it was a small group: Paulo Verdoccia, Julie, and Carl Daffin, the company's chief bioinformatics architect. Carl was one of those scary smart types who could solve just about any kind of scientific problem. He also had the unusual ability to communicate with people, not just computers. He'd once said in a meeting with the firm's younger staff, "This report is a tad janky. I used to crunch these factor analysis models by hand with an old HP calculator, and your results don't match the write-up. Go back and rerun the whole analysis and then rewrite your results, conclusions, and recommendations. I shouldn't have to tell you this sort of thing. You should know better. We're not in grad school anymore, kids. Get your act together." No one had held it against him.

Julie looked quickly at Carl as she entered the room and remembered precisely why he was also known in his younger years as a ladies' man. She admired his tall, thin physique, and his bright, penetrating, nearly mesmerizing blue eyes. She loved his flare and sense of style. *He is one attention-getting human specimen*, Julie thought.

Carl had a good vibe, good looks, and a great rap. He drove a flashy Aston Martin and always had loud rock or funky music blasting as he drove into the company's parking lot. He did it as a fashion statement. He knew how gifted and unique he was and took every opportunity to strut his stuff. Many scientists couldn't string together three complete normal sentences, much less convince a group of business people or politicians about the virtues of a scientific concept or hypothesis. Carl could almost hypnotize a crowd. He was a rare man indeed, a poet and a brilliant scientist in the skin of an Adonis. And although he was a genius and Paulo's right hand man, Carl had no clue what he was about to hear.

Julie surmised that the meeting involved one of Paulo's high-level government contacts and was potentially a fast-track project. That usually meant lots of money. The company had enjoyed many such projects before. They had developed a reputation for discreetly fulfilling their obligations and delivering high value biotechnology results in record time; their success had been meteoric. Their services were never cheap, but the deliverables were matchless.

Paulo, Carl, and an unknown man were standing in a close circle when Julie entered the room.

"Dr. Perthuis, meet Dr. Mike Reynolds," Paulo said.

"Dr. Perthuis, it is a pleasure to meet you, ma'am. I've read a lot of your work. Very impressive indeed," Dr. Reynolds said as he extended his hand to shake hers.

He then handed Julie one of his business cards. It read simply:

T. Michael Reynolds

Senior Director, Special Projects

Bellihurton, Inc.

201.604.5758

Julie recognized a cell phone number when she saw one; the clandestine air thickened like fog and she knew already that relevant information about this Reynolds character would not be popping up like mushrooms in a Google search.

"Dr. Reynolds has been given an unusual and special assignment from Bellihurton," Paulo said, "and we are looking forward to hearing about it."

"I'm curious," Carl said "The sooner we get started, the better."

"Thank you Dr. Daffin, you are so right. Let's get started," Reynolds said with an insincere smile. "Please call me Mike."

Reynolds did not appear to have much of a personality. He faked an easy-going manner, gracious and polite, but he was strictly business. His military haircut, dark grey suit, white button-down shirt and a subdued red, white, and blue striped tie would allow him to fade into any group of professionally dressed men. He had perfected a perfectly bland image.

"Let's take a seat," Paulo said.

As Mike began speaking, his tone became a bit more serious, a bit on the dour side. His Southern demeanor softened what otherwise would have had an edge, however. "Thanks, Paulo and thank you also, Julie and Carl. You are about to become part of a very important project. I am required to emphasize that each of us is operating under the aegis of the Patriot Act, and as such, everything you discuss, think about, wake-up in the middle of the night worrying about, is strictly confidential and TS classified."

He took a pause and a sip of water and quickly eyeballed each of them to see if he thought he'd have a problem. "The company, and specifically the three of you, is part of a new mission to improve the protection of our domestic security interests. The mission is code-named "Deep Thought." You are working for Bellihurton, not the Department of Defense. Not the Psy-Ops Division. Not the CIA. You are working for a contractor. Are there any questions?" he asked rhetorically. "Am I perfectly clear?"

Julie thought, *We are now working as subcontractors to another subcontractor that is being funded by the some branch of the Feder-*

al Government.. It's gotta be the PsyOps Department of the United States Army. She also thought, *I don't think I like where this is going. I don't think I like this guy."*

T. Michael Reynolds was born and raised in Arkansas. Arkansas didn't have a reputation for producing lots of smart guys, but the ones they did produce were really smart. Stevens, Walton, Clinton; all pretty smart guys, like 'em or not. "T Mike" as his old boy buddies called him, fell into this category. T Mike was a graduate of the University of Texas, summa cum laude in biology, and held a PhD in genetics and a law degree from Vanderbilt. T Mike had strong southern Baptist religious values and a rock-solid education. He'd done his thesis on McClintock's "gene jumping" theory. He had been interested in genetics since the age of eleven, replicating all of Gregor Mendel's experiments in his own backyard garden by the age of fourteen. It was T Mike's early and deeply religious thinking that had originally introduced him to Mendel and the field of genetics. T Mike was studying the history of religion and came across the writings of Mendel. One thing led to another and T Mike became an ardent student of genetics, and like its early founder, pursued his work under the cross.

In rarified southern religious corners it's a very small world and it wasn't long before T Mike and Arkloft were introduced. They were each cut from the same cloth. T Mike quickly and easily supported the fire and brimstone of Arkloft's fundamentalist doctrine.

Now in the hyper-secure room of HGMP, Reynolds continued with their meeting.

"I need to warn you that the information you are about to see on video is not only secret, but disturbing," Mike said, now with the tone of a concerned father.

Carl tried to catch Julie's eye but missed it. He was thinking, *This guy's full of shit.*

The room dimmed and a video with a voice over began to run. After watching for a few minutes, Julie concluded the video content was nothing new, the same roundup of anti-American footage that the network media had been broadcasting for the past few years.

The significant difference, however, she conceded, was that the pictures were all ostensibly taken on American soil. The storyline was the increasing acceptance by naturalized US citizens of terrorist views, here on US property. Despite the clinical patina of "facts," there were no solid statistics, Julie noticed immediately; it was simply an extremely well-constructed message of fear. There were scenes of schools, churches, high school football stadiums, dance halls, bars, and large rock concert gatherings. Julie noticed that backpacks were photographed frequently, as were gays, and kids with long hair, earrings, and tattoos. The footage of Mexicans and Arabs was subtly, cleverly, and convincingly woven into the message fabric. It was just overt enough.

The three scientists in the room watching the video were highly trained and extremely skilled observers. They counted everything they saw. They were trained to count. That's what scientists and researchers did. They counted things and compared them. They calculated frequencies, proportions, central tendencies, and standard deviations in their heads if for no other reason than to keep from getting bored. The bias in the presentation was obvious and unavoidable.

When the film was over and the room's lighting was brought back to normal, Reynolds took the floor. "This is why we need your help. I am not sure how else to really describe it, but we need to be able to see better. We need to be able to see within these increasingly dangerous groups. We need to be able to see within and with much greater clarity. Some of these groups have ties to known insurgents. We are now in an era of constant and significant threats to our way of life and our national security. The insurgents have penetrated our communities, our schools, and even our churches."

How overused the term insurgents had become! Julie thought. *Everyone had insurgents these days. There were insurgents in the Republican Party, insurgents in the business community, and insurgents in the church. These newcomers into their respective areas used to be called "new entrants." Now they were called insurgents. Ridiculous.*

Julie quickly glanced over to Paulo and thought, *Paulo deserves his money and I'm glad I don't have his job. To have to deal with the political forces and steer company governance in an environment of fast-paced change was no mean feat. Paulo looked so calm and dispassionate as he listened. Nice sport coat,* she thought. *Looks like a silk and linen blend. One of my favorites and in a nice tight tweed. He must have picked that up in Italy.*

While Julie was distracting herself, Reynolds rattled on. "We have lost our ability to identify the enemy with sufficient reliability. They now look and act like *real* Americans, but they think like the enemy. They have infiltrated our society. We know most of the people we observe are well intentioned, but sadly, an increasing number are not. So, we need to sharpen, we need to enhance our perceptual abilities. We not only want to be able to see farther, hear better and smell better, but without the aid of mechanical tools. We need the ability to *sense* better. We need to be able to perceive more. We need new doors into the mind and their keys to allow us to go down new, yet to be used, mental or psychic hallways. We need to get inside these groups' or individual's heads and make sure we don't trigger suspicion or resentment. We want to avoid awareness and, of course, civil disobedience at all costs."

As he spoke, Reynolds's eyes flickered over each of the three scientist's faces in turn, as if on a timer. It was clear that his audience was not as rapt and convinced as he'd hoped. Indeed, the Perthuis woman didn't even appear to be paying attention. He continued, "*Deep Thought* is about genetically or chemically altering our ability to perceive individual thought. We are hiring HGMP to develop and sequence a process that will allow us to manage this chemically and biologically, and on demand. We want HGMP to synthesize or otherwise create a substance so that it can be used, at will, in the interest of national and domestic security. We want a new chemical agent. We need to have this in hand, along with the experimental protocols, trial outcomes, and process methods and formulas, in four months. We acknowledge that the product will necessarily still be technically experimental in nature, but that the deployment probability is high, nonetheless. There will be no government agencies involved in this project whatsoever. There will be no other subcontractors except you. All decisions and communications you may have with the government regarding licenses, supplies, waivers, and so forth, without exception, will be conducted directly through me. Are there any questions?"

The room was silent for fifteen seconds, which is a long time for four people to remain speechless. The three friends looked at one another, their decision written on their silent faces.

Then Paulo said, "Mr. Reynolds, HGMP is honored to be considered for this project, but we don't have the resources for something of this scope, and the time line you have provided seems at first glance very ambitious. I know we have done business in the past, and have a number of ongoing projects with Bellihurton, but I don't see how we could undertake something of this scope given this timeline. My instincts incline me to bow out of this invitation, but by extending the utmost gratitude to you and your associates for having the confidence in our firm. We are honored to have been considered for this groundbreaking and important undertaking."

"Mr. Verdoccia, this contract is being offered to one firm and one firm only. Yours. It is an off-budget, no-bid, no-contest contract. I don't have to remind you of your other ongoing government work and the work you are doing directly for Bellihurton. Moreover, this is an unusually rich contract; twenty-five million dollars in advance and twenty-five million upon completion if done within the four month time period and without leaks. My recommendation is that you and your colleagues take a sidebar and come back with your decision. Please take a few minutes to talk amongst yourselves. I'll wait."

On that note, the three HGMP folks left the room and went down the hall to another secure meeting room. Paulo closed the door and said, "So, what do you think?

Carl spoke first. "This guy is a fucking creep. He wants us to create some kind of mindreading potion so the Feds can find guys they don't like? Paulo, we have a great business here, we're trying to find the cure for cancer for Christ's sake, but this project, its scope and goals, is *way* over the line. Let me be very clear, this is bullshit."

Julie chimed in, "I agree with Carl, the guy gives me the hebejebes, but he has made *their* position very clear. Remember Charles Colson, one of Nixon's hatchet men lawyers? He had a slogan behind his desk that read; *When you've got 'em by the balls, their hearts and minds will follow.* I feel as if we're in one of the Godfather films. We've just been made an offer we can't refuse. We will probably be professionally and financially destroyed. But at least we'll get to keep our souls."

Paulo wrapped it up and said, "Yes this guy is very intimidating, if not creepy. The project violates my sensitivities as a human being and as an American. Julie is correct."

They returned to the presentation room and let Mr. Reynolds know how pleased they were to have been considered, but they agreed that they were not able take on this extremely ambitious project.

Without a missing beat and with no visible reaction, Mr. Reynolds said, "Very well. It has been my pleasure to meet each of you. I wish you the very best of luck. Now Mr. Verdoccia, if you would walk me out, I would appreciate it." On that note, the meeting was over.

Julie said, "Mike, thanks for this unique opportunity. I am sorry it won't work out. By the way, where did you get that tie? My husband would love that."

"Thank you. You are as charming as I've been told. Frankly, I am not sure about the tie. One of my staff had it made for me. I'll have them send one for Clark," Mike said.

"Thanks Mike, that's very thoughtful of you," Julie replied, belatedly realizing that he had referred to her husband by his name.

"Oh, and I'll have someone send something to your two handsome sons. Peter and Philip, right?"

Julie's breath caught in her chest as she felt an unseen noose tighten around her. And when she saw the looks on the faces of her colleagues, she knew they felt it, too.

Chapter Eight

After Reynolds had left, they had the room re-swept for bugs. As a result of this precautionary activity, the three of them kept their conversation explicitly vague, and spoke more about the financial rewards and rigors of the timetable than anything else. Just because they didn't find any bugs didn't necessarily mean there weren't any. As in most technology fields, there had been radical advances in the last five years, particularly in the field of communications surveillance. For all they knew, Reynolds could have sprayed some top-secret defense department nanocloud in the room. They didn't find evidence of anything, but just to be on the safe side, they decided to take a walk into the company's campus grounds for a follow-up conversation.

What they didn't know, and the same could be said about Bellihurton, was that their activities were being closely watched, scrutinized and files were being copied and prepared for global release. Depending upon one's perspective, the much-lauded or much-despised organization of Wikileaks was bird-dogging each of these organizations and had been for years. Ironically, Julie's earlier thoughts about Wikileaks were actually in the works. Julie was now an unwitting participant in two projects; each secret and each serving diametrically different ends of the political and social systems.

Among Wikileaks' ranks was arguably the world's brightest and most creative programmer and systems hacker, the mild-mannered and nondescript John Galt. Unbeknownst to John's parents they had been extremely prescient in naming their son.

As the three strolled on the company campus, Paulo, being the consummate executive, waited for either Carl or Julie to talk first.

Carl was still pissed. In a polite but an angry tone, he said, "Paulo, I felt pretty blind-sided in there. You had to know more about that than we did. Why didn't we get a heads up?"

Paulo responded, "Carl and Julie, believe me or not, I was just as much in the dark on this as you were. I received a call from the California attorney general, my friend Jim Duckworth. He said I would be receiving a call from the secret services area of the Justice Department. Jim said he didn't even know the individual's name, but said the matter was urgent, involving national security, and that I should clear my calendar. That was it. The call from Reynolds came in, last Thursday, and then I called you and scheduled the meeting we just had. The rest you know.

"The application is obviously questionable, but by not accepting the project, I'm quite certain that three things will happen. First, the contract will be awarded to Aptech or Mapgen, or some other firm. Second, all of our government contracts will be terminated. Third, the Justice Department will figure out a way to destroy our business and in all likelihood, our personal lives. We are familiar with their political convictions and their enforcement techniques. To put a very sharp point on it, we have been let in on a very nefarious plan. It seems quite naïve to think we could just say, 'Thanks for sharing your darkest illegal and immoral plan, but we're going to pass. But thanks for thinking of us.' Are we ready for that?"

Carl and Julie knew each other well, very well. During their twenties, they had a short-lived but heated romance in Mexico. Carl was hitchhiking around the country and ended up one night bedless in the beautiful town of Oaxaca, a lovely mountain town with a famous market. Oaxaca had its own unique black pottery and excellent Zapotec ruins. Carl neglected to take into account the effect a summer religious event, the Guelaguetza, or Los Lunes del Cerro, would have on room availability for his sleeping accommodations. Everything was sold out.

Carl was in a café deciding which park bench to use as a bed for the night when Julie approached him and said, "Hey, I'm guessing you're out in the cold for the night. Care to join us at our campsite?" Julie was traveling with three other women, but they had two cars. Actually, Julie's was a pickup with a sleeping compartment over the back.

Carl stood up and said, "Sure, are you kidding? A beautiful woman approaches me at the end of the night and invites me to share a desperately needed place to sleep. I now feel like the luckiest man alive. I am fully packed and ready to go. My name is Carl. Care for a coffee or anything?"

"My name is Julie," she said. "I'll pass on the coffee, thanks, but we have other stuff to drink back at the camp site."

Julie and Carl hit it off. They drank tequila around the campfire and then rocked the night away, into the next morning, the next evening, and for the next two weeks. They trekked through ruins, bought textiles and ate food at the markets. They also tried 'shrooms for the first time. They found a local kid named Eduardo who know where the 'shrooms grew. Eduardo took them to the cow pastures early in the morning after a rain and pointed out the ones they should eat. Carl and Julie would reach down and pinch off the mushroom's stem just above the cow paddy and pop them in their mouths. Within a few minutes they were transported to another reality. This was a seminal experience for them both. They joked later that the cows have a good reason to be classified as sacred. If this was part of their purpose, they were indeed very special creatures. Their views of the world and the vastness of the universe were forever changed.

Julie and Carl had a wonderful time together in every way, sexually, intellectually, experientially, but the vacation ended and Carl returned to the States. A few weeks later, Julie did the same. They connected once again for a romp during one of Julie's travels, but stateside, for whatever reason, the relationship never solidified. They parted very good and special friends with shared memories of a truly magical episode in their lives. They occasionally shot one another post cards if they were somewhere that triggered a thought of the other.

Eventually Julie met Clark and they were married. Carl met his wife-to-be and did the same. Years later, and quite by accident, they each ended up at HGMP. Carl was already there when Julie arrived. They worked well together and agreed they should not revisit their days together in the sack. That was then and this was now. They'd had a glorious time together, but their romantic relationship was destined to be left in its proper place, the past.

Julie thought as she walked back to her office, *Serendipity is a funny thing, however, and HGMP's refusal of this project had been influenced by the shared experiences Julie and Carl had while they were in Mexico.*

Chapter Nine

When Julie returned to her office and thought about the implications of Project Deep Thought. *Jesus Christ*, she first thought, *who the fuck comes up with these stupid code names? Do they have a special team spending taxpayer dollars that churns out goofy project names just in case they need one? Deep Thought. Give me a Goddamned break!*. She laughed to herself thinking the project name's author was either a fan of Watergate or Linda Lovelace. She hoped it was at least the latter.

Julie worked because she needed the intellectual stimulation and challenge. She and her family had more money than they could ever spend, but they were relatively frugal and thoughtful about money and did not want to distort Philip's and Peter's views of the world by flaunting their good fortune. They drove nice cars and had a nice home, but nothing was over the top. Some of the stuff in the Valley was way, *way* over the top.

Even though she and Clark had money, Julie couldn't help but think about her potential bonus. Money is funny that way. With Julie's performance incentive plan, she probably would have taken home another three and a half million bucks. Not too shabby for

four months or so of work. Money was now just a game and intellectual exercise.

Oh, well, she didn't want blood money. Sitting at her desk, she
eyed the sphere again and thought, *things have a way of coming
back around.*

She had backlog of e-mails, the message light was blinking on
her phone, and her secretary had fielded a number of urgent calls.
As far as she was concerned, there was only one urgent call, and that
was to Pachita, their on-and-off-again caregiver and housekeeper.

Pachita had been all but a grandmother to the boys when they
were younger, but now that they were older and Julie's schedule
was more manageable, she was drifting away by degrees. Now,
she wanted to hear Pachita's sweet, familiar voice tell her that the
boys were there with her. Safe.

Chapter Ten

A t three in the afternoon Julie was pacing her office, looking at the campus through her floor-to-ceiling window, waiting to hear from Pachita, who, she assumed, she hoped, was picking the boys up from school. She was still stuck on the meeting with Reynolds and the overreaching temerity of the project he proposed. *What has our country become?* she thought. A little spying, she understood reluctantly, is probably necessary, but this psychological and moral profiling was so far over the line it made her sick to her stomach. And to be dragged into it was unthinkable. She took a long drink of water to dilute the stomach acid she could feel building. She wanted to discuss her thoughts and feelings with Clark, but she knew it was out of the question. She and Clark had reached an understanding years ago to not discuss her high-security projects.

Across town, Clark's office phone rang. "Good afternoon, pediatric practice. This is Janice," said the attractive voice.

"Good afternoon. This is Lieutenant Forest McCants of the United States Navy. May I speak with Dr. Perthuis please? Dr.

Julie Perthuis asked me to give the doctor a call," said a polite and authoritative voice.

"Is Dr. Perthuis expecting your call, Lieutenant McCants?" asked the receptionist.

"I don't know, frankly," said the Lieutenant. "But I'm sure he would like to honor his wife's request."

"Okay," said the receptionist. "Let me see if Dr. Perthuis is available."

Clark was wrapping up his day, slogging through some files for billing purposes. The paperwork was really irritating. All Clark wanted to do was practice medicine, but these days he spent about a third of his time just keeping his records in order. When his in-office line rang, he noticed the time was 3:37.

"Yep, Janice. What do you need?" Clark said.

"I have a Lieutenant McCants from the Navy on the phone. He said that Julie asked him to call you. Should I put him through?" she asked.

"Did he say what he wanted?" Clark asked.

"No. He just said that your wife had asked him to call."

"All right, put him through," instructed Clark.

"Dr. Perthuis, this is Lieutenant Forest McCants. Your wife asked me to give you a call. She has arranged a field trip for you and your sons and didn't want to alarm you when we just showed up. She has engineered quite a nice little treat for you and your boys," said the lieutenant.

"What are you talking about?" Clark asked in an irritated, incredulous voice. "She didn't mention this to me."

"She wanted it to be a surprise. Give her a ring. I know she wants this to be a surprise, but I'm sure she would be happy to allay any concerns and confirm our outing," said the lieutenant.

"Lieutenant, I think I'll do that. I'm going to put you on hold."

Clark said abruptly. He hit the speed dial for Julie's cell phone. It rang three times and then Clark heard Julie's voice.

"Hi. I'm in a meeting, but I'll bet you're calling about Forest McCants," Julie said in a soft voice.

"Well, yeah," Clark said, half curious, half annoyed. "What's up?"

"I'll fill you in later, but we're taking on a new project and I was able to arrange a cool trip for you, Philip, and Peter. You will like this Lieutenant McCants. He is super-nice and has put together a wonderful itinerary. I'm sorry I can't join you, but it will be an ideal time for you and the boys to have some serious male bonding on Uncle Sam's nickel. The one thing you don't have to worry about is being safe. These are your kind of guys. The Navy's finest. I've got to go, Hon. You guys enjoy yourselves. I'll see you later. Love you."

"You too," said Clark. Clark hit the hold button and resumed his conversation with Lieutenant McCants.

"All right. I'm ready," Clark said.

"Perfect," replied the lieutenant.

"I'm in your lot. Come out whenever you're ready and we'll head over and pick up your boys. I'm in a grey Lincoln Town Car. Take your time. There's no rush," said the lieutenant convincingly.

Unbeknownst to Clark, Reynolds's men had sampled Julie's voice earlier in the day and had created a digital version. When Clark hit the speed dial, the call was captured and routed to a recording studio. In the studio was a man about thirty years old, an actor who did voice-overs for a living. His ponytail fell over the back of his T-shirt. His over-ear headphones had an attached microphone. When he read his script, he did it in the character of a wife and concerned mother, and a mother who was in an open meeting and didn't have a lot of time. His voice was smooth and calm; at times almost a whisper. His male voice went into the microphone, and at the other end, Clark heard the reassuring voice of Julie. Julie, none the wiser, still paced and gazed out the window of her office.

Clark walked out to the office parking lot and there was a nondescript grey Town Car. A fit-looking, forty-something officer got out of the car and extended his hand to Clark.

"Dr. Perthuis, Lieutenant Forest McCants. Nice to meet you, sir," said the lieutenant.

"Nice to meet you also," Clark replied.

The lieutenant opened the door and Clark slid into the back seat and put his briefcase on the seat next to him. The lieutenant closed Clark's door and then got behind the wheel and closed the driver's door.

"You're wife has done a very nice thing for you and your sons. You guys are going to love this. I do these so-called field trips for a living and I never get tired of them. It's thrilling to see all of the things you are going to see. You also get to see the pride of the United States Armed Forces at work. I'm referring to the Navy, of course, sir," said the lieutenant with a laugh. "We think we're the best of the group, and I'm not embarrassed to say so."

"Dr. Perthuis told us Philip and Peter should be home from school now, so let's swing by your house, pick them up and then be on our way. Okay, sir?" asked the lieutenant.

"Sure," Clark replied.

When they pulled into the driveway, Philip and Peter had either been primed or had seen the car. Clark got out and both boys jumped into his arms, almost knocking him over.

"Hey guys! Easy does it. It's not football season yet. Are you ready for a way-cool field trip? Your mother has cooked up some big surprise for us. Supposed to be really special. This is Lieutenant McCants. He's going to be our tour guide. Are you guys set? Need anything before we head off?" Clark asked.

"We're set," said Peter.

"Me too," said Philip.

"Okay, let me quickly change clothes and tell Pachita she can go home. I'll be right back."

Clark, Philip, and Peter climbed into the back of the Town Car. The lieutenant kept looking at them through the rearview mirror, cracking silly knock-knock and light bulb jokes. The boys took to him easily as they headed onto the expressway.

"We're about ten minutes from SJC," the lieutenant said into his cell phone.

Ahead of their car by about twenty cars was a security detail consisting of a white van with large lettered messaging on the side, *Mark and Sons Painting. Licensed and Bonded since 1976.* In addition to the van were two Harley Softtails with biker types riding them side by side in one lane. They were Special Forces personnel in costume. Behind them was another detail consisting of a Black Suburban and two other motorcycles, a Ducati Monstar S4R and a BMW K1600 GTL. Each was black, one following the other. One driver looked like an Asian hipster and the other one like a businessman going home from work.

When they pulled into San Jose International Airport they went directly into a special area. The Town Car pulled directly up to a large Merlin helicopter. Clark, Philip, and Peter were wide-eyed when Lieutenant McCants opened their door and they walked onto the tarmac.

"Pretty cool, huh, kids?" said the lieutenant

By this time Clark and the boys believed that Lieutenant Mc-Cants was their very best friend and one of the coolest guys they had ever met. McCants was really good at what he did. With an easy smile, stupid jokes, and a crisp military uniform, he was both disarming and comforting.

"So, let's go for a spin shall we? You're gonna love this," McCants said enthusiastically.

They climbed the steep metal stairs; each took a seat as instructed by another man in a military uniform. The door was pulled shut as the big blade above their heads began to spin. In a minute or so, they were rising in the air. The chopper took a steep turn, more to get his passengers excited than anything, and up they went, heading out to the coast toward the Bay. In the distance they saw the Golden Gate Bridge. The spectacular expanse was grand enough from a distance, but when the chopper flew under it, the three passengers almost jumped out of their seats. The helicopter swung inland to see some of the renowned hills of San Francisco and the striking cityscape: Fisherman's Wharf, Candlestick Park, AT&T Park. They could even see the game from the air; the Giants' broadcast was pumped into their earphones. Clark and the boys looked at each other with huge smiles and wonder in their eyes. Then they flew over Telegraph Hill and the financial district with the famous Transamerica Pyramid.

After viewing the city, they turned around and hovered over Alcatraz Island. They were close enough to land on the abandoned prison. The next stop would be Goat Island, announced the pilot. "This 116-acre island is about two miles northeast of the city," the pilot droned. "It was established in 1868 and served as a regular army camp until 1880, when the island was transferred to the Navy Department. There are old barracks and of course, goats. If you look down to the right, you can see them."

The goats scattered as the noise of the approaching chopper frightened them. The pilot wanted to show just how much power and speed his craft had, so he continued west. When they were fifteen minutes out, the coast was a distant view. "Okay, everyone, now for the high point of our trip. Make sure your seatbelts are tightened. Sergeant Lopez is going to check just to make sure. After he gives me the go-ahead, we're going to open up the side of the helicopter. It will take your breath away, so get ready. Here we go."

The side of the chopper opened and Clark, Philip, and Peter were basically sitting on the edge of a fast moving chopper, six thousand feet in the air and very far out at sea. Their shrieks couldn't be heard above the whine of the blades.

Julie, working at her desk, felt her phone vibrate. She opened it and read the message from Clark. "Please open this link. Great gift. Love, Clark."

How weird, Julie thought. *Clark's not a check-out-this-link kind of guy.*

She clicked the link and it took her to a live video feed. She was looking at a flying helicopter with its side door open. Julie knew a little bit about choppers from a government project she'd been involved with years ago. This was an EH101 Merlin HMS Monmouth used for transporting troops. As she looked at the chopper, a camera operator panned the chopper and the sea below. The chopper appeared to be about four to five thousand feet in the air. As the camera panned the area, it was obvious there wasn't anything for fifty or a hundred miles. She saw the coastline of California in the distance.

Then, a second camera feed began. This camera was trained on a camera operator riding in a Westland Apache WAH-64D Longbow. The camera operator zoomed in to show the Apache with a tight shot. Julie saw the aviator sunglasses of the pilot and the bearded cameraman pointing his camera out the window.

The feed then switched back to the EH101 and zoomed in on

the open door. As the image of the door became sharper she saw Clark, Peter, and Philip, all sitting on a bench a few feet back from the door. They each had green over-the-ear headsets with microphones. They looked very excited. She saw Peter's face. He was wide-eyed and staring out through the large opening on the side of the chopper. Then a voice came on. Although there was ambient noise from the chopper, the audio quality was pretty good.

A guy in a military uniform and aviator sunglasses walked over to Peter and said,

"Hey Peter, this is really fun, huh? Want to throw some stuff into the ocean? I have some fun things. Want to try a tomato or a melon?"

"Sure. Let's throw some melons," Peter said.

The soldier said, "Let me make sure you're buckle is secure and tight. I don't want you falling out."

"Me either!" said Peter with a nervous laugh.

The helicopter abruptly dove toward the water, and Julie could hear her husband and sons gasp. She felt faint. She tried to make her fingers stop trembling long enough to IM Carl and Paulo.

"Relax," laughed the soldier, "we're just getting close enough to see the melon explode." He checked the buckle and its tether to the bench and then asked Peter to join him at the opening. As Peter was standing at the edge of the open door, the soldier handed him a small watermelon.

"Okay, Peter, chuck it and watch it fall," instructed the soldier.

Peter underhanded the melon into space and the camera in the Apache chopper camera followed its descent. When the melon hit the surface of the water, it made an enormous, satisfying crater.

"Pretty cool, huh!" exclaimed the soldier. "Wanna throw some more stuff? I love doing this! I could do this all day, but my boss won't let me. You guys are lucky."

The soldier then turned to Philip and asked, "How about you

Philip, want to throw some stuff into the ocean? I don't want to throw too much as we get close to shore because it's like throwing garbage into the water. But out here, it really doesn't matter. The big fish eat whatever comes their way and then the stuff is gone."

"Sure," Philip said excitedly.

Carol and Paulo burst into Julie's office and saw their friend in tears. She motioned to them and they drew around her to watch her screen.

The soldier was checking all of Philip's buckles and tethers. Philip did the same. After Philip was done, the soldier turned to Clark and asked, "Doctor, would you like to speak to your wife? She's been watching the whole show and I am sure very happy to see you guys enjoying yourselves so much."

"Absolutely," said Clark. "My wife never ceases to amaze me."

"Just speak into the headset. It's connected to the video feed your wife has been watching."

"Hon, you've outdone yourself with this little stunt. I really wish you had told me, but I understand the surprise. These Navy guys are impressive—polite, professional. Even you would like them! Too bad you couldn't come. Thank Paulo for me. I'm guessing he had a hand in this too. See you in a couple of hours. Thanks, kiddo. This is really great," Clark said as he signed off.

Then the camera focused on the soldier's face. He looked directly into it, switched a button on his headset and then said, "Dr. Perthuis. We've set-up a two-way communication line for your ears only. If you would press the speaker icon on your iPhone you'll be all set. I'm signing off."

Reynolds said, "Hello, Julie. I hope we didn't startle you too much. I just wanted—"

Julie interrupted him mid-sentence and said, "You fucking piece of shit. If you do anything to my family—"

Reynolds hissed. "You'll do what, doctor, call the police? Call the FBI? Go ahead and see where it gets you. If I weren't a family man myself I'd have had all three of them tossed out of the chopper, never to be seen or heard from again. But then if I'd done that you would have been distracted from the work you need to get done. Get with the program. You know too much now to walk away. We want only you, so put your moral righteousness and political indignation aside and focus. The situation in our country is grave. Sorry for the pun and double entendre, but gravity is not a laughing matter in this case. Let's connect at the end of the week. Sorry again for the pressure, but we're in the business of getting things done."

The line went dead.

Chapter Eleven

"So, I guess our plans have changed," Paulo said. "Some are born evil, some achieve evil, and some..."

"Have evil thrust upon them," Carl finished.

Julie couldn't speak. She could hardly breathe.

Julie's first call was to Clark, a primary care family physician in a small practice with three other doctors. They had a well-established practice in the area. Clark called it EM², "Easily Manageable Medicine"—lots of flu, strawberries from sliding into second base and occasional food poisoning from questionable sushi. It was a pretty good gig as far as gigs go.

Julie pressed the speed dial on her desk phone and Clark's cell phone rang. When he finally picked up—this was at least her eighteenth try in as many minutes—she felt her knees weaken.

"Hi. Where are you?" she said, willing herself to sound cheerful. "Have a minute?"

"Sure Babydoll. For you, anytime. What's up?" Clark said.

"Are you okay? Are the boys with you? Is everyone okay?" Her voice was pressured and she struggled not to burst into tears with the relief of hearing his voice.

"We're fine, we had a great time," Clark assured her. "It looked much scarier than it was."

Oh, you have no idea, Julie thought. She pressed her fingers to her temples and nodded. "I'm so glad." Her voice still shook.

"You, on the other hand, don't sound so good," Clark said.

"I've got some interesting news; it's of the good news/bad news type."

"You've got my attention," he said, "your choice on a or b."

"I'll give you the good news first," she said "There's a pretty good chance I'm going to get three and a half million bucks on top of what I was expecting to earn this year."

There was a moment of silence.

"Clark, are you there?" Julie asked.

"Are you shitting me?" he said.

"Nope," she replied. "I shit you not. Now, for the bad news. We're probably not going to have sex for the next four months, or for that matter, see much of each other. I'm now staring down the barrel of sixteen back-to-back consecutive work weeks from hell."

"What's the project?" Clark asked.

"If I told you I would *truly* have to kill you, or somebody else would for sure. So just don't ask. Really," Julie replied, her breathing more even now that she knew her family was safe and she could turn to practical matters. "Are you going to be okay with this?"

Clark responded quickly, "I'll tell you after tonight, you sexy animal, if you catch my drift."

"Yeah, yeah, I catch it, big fella. And you are so lucky to have such a sexy animal," Julie said with a laugh in her voice. "We'll make it a night to remember. I'll put on my sexual creativity hat and you do the same."

"Roger Wilco," said Clark with excitement in his voice. "I'll remain seventeen in my libido as long as my body holds out."

"Outstanding! Would you mind picking up the boys?" she replied. "I need to offload all of my current projects and reorganize my work here. I really want to get a quick leg up on this new mofo of an assignment today before the world as I've known it comes to an abrupt end for the next four months."

"Not a problem baby doll, I'll see if Bradley can pick up my afternoon appointments. How about some Italian food for dinner?" Clark asked. "I'll grab that as well."

"You're the best," Julie said. "See you around seven thirty."

After offloading all of her previously scheduled work, Julie began to outline the scope of Deep Thought. First on her list was to give the project a name she could use with a straight face. She was going to call it "4.20" for the moment. Those numbers corresponded to the ordinal positions of D and T in the alphabet. *No need to get melodramatic about these things*, Julie thought. *It's just a fucking project, for Christ's sake.*

Julie cleared her calendar for the next four months. Completing this would take a full day of meetings and a lot of fast hand-offs, but then the deck would be clear so a project plan could be conceived, drafted, vetted, and scheduled. They didn't have much to go on. They were supposed to help the government creeps read minds, more or less. That was the gist of it. The concept was fucked-up, but as she had persuaded others, she was now persuading herself—she really did not have a choice. It was one of those "either do it or die" propositions. She recalled a line she had heard in a movie; that "rationalization was much more important than sex, you can get through a day without sex, but you cannot get through a day without rationalization." Truer words were never said. Julie again tried to reassure herself that something good could come out of it.

She gazed at the sphere in the bright light of the late afternoon sun and then closed her eyes to reflect on the project. There are many factors that influence perception, but in the final analysis it is all about wavelengths and wavelength perception. Everything emits and receives or reflects electromagnetic wavelengths. Everything has some level of inherent vibration. Crystalline material is a common example of non-biological matter that emits and reflects wavelengths. The electromagnetic wavelength area was logically the place to start. If the goal is to "see better" as it were, the perceptual spectra needed to be expanded or enhanced in some fashion. The goal was to have improved sensory awareness and that had to involve extra-sensitive perception. The research paradigm had to incorporate the use of wavelengths in its design.

Julie opened her eyes, and jotted a few quick notes on a yellow pad. Although she lived and worked in the Mecca of all things digital, she still liked yellow pads. They were sort of a journal for her, with random thoughts, dates, to do lists, scribbles. She had hundreds of them in storage from decades of work. She was always surprised at how often they came in handy.

She backed up her current files, logged off her system, and left to meet Clark and the boys for dinner. This would be the beginning of the last night of being a normal wife and mother. The next four months were going to be wild. She felt exhilarated, challenged, chagrined. And afraid.

Julie, Clark, and the kids had a cozy family meal that evening. The food was terrific, much of it lost on the young boys, but the pasta was fresh and the sauces were superb. One benefit of the Bay Area and the Valley is that there was fierce competition in the restaurant business. It didn't take much effort to find a truly fine meal. Peter was a fan of Italian styled ragout, particularly the rich duck ragout. As they ate, they talked about food, school, sports, video games, and the boys' favorite comedy and music videos. Toward the end, Julie told the boys that their government had given her a really big and important assignment, and that it was super-secret! It was so secret that Julie didn't even know what it was all about. Julie also passed along the good and bad news.

The bad news was that she would be very busy for the next four months and wouldn't see the family as much as everyone would like, particularly her. The good news was that their abuelita, Pachita, would be around, making them the foods they really liked—chocolate milk, rice and beans, tacos de pollo, and mangos on a stick. The little boys almost yelped with glee.

Clark, on the other hand, was losing a wife and a lover and saw the writing on the wall. He had a second martini that night and Julie finished a bottle of Pinot Noir. That got them primed for some aggressive sex. Julie was still pissed and freaked out by what had happened and planned to take out her angst and frustration on her husband in the sack. *He'll be wondering what's gotten in to me*, she thought. They both knew that there was not going to be any regular romping for a good sixteen weeks.

Julie and Clark had a good time that night. After the boys were in bed, they talked. Clark probed for some insight on the super-secret project but didn't get very far.

Julie finally said, "You can poke around on what I'm doing at work, or you can poke me, but I'm running out of energy. Is this your idea of sexual creativity? So, do I need to quote Marvin Gaye or what?" She had a way of cutting to the chase.

And it was a good and memorable romp. They were each

pleased with each other's creativity and appetites. They hadn't banged that rewardingly for a while.

After they were worn out, they drifted off.

Julie's sleep was as fitful as a convict's the night before sentencing. She drifted in and out of dream state almost as if she was under the influence of 'shrooms. Sometimes she wasn't sure if she was dreaming or awake. It was as if she was bouncing between stage two and stage three sleep. Some of the images were vivid and startling. Most were forgotten. She'd drift off into the past, then the future. She was in college, then in the birthing room with Philip. She was in the birthing room with Peter. She was in Mexico. She saw images of war. She saw images of peace. She saw Hiroshima. She saw cows. She saw the clock that said 4:20 in green LEDs. She thought, *I hope I'm dreaming or this is really weird.* Finally, around 4:30, she got some sorely needed deep sleep.

Chapter Twelve

When Julie arrived at her office the next morning, she felt a bit fatigued from a less than perfect sleep, but she also had a newfound energy. She was resigned to the big new gig. She felt, somehow, that she was zeroing in on an idea, a conceptual framework for her project, but the gestalt wasn't fully formed. It was like the leaves turning upside down on a bright sunny day and knowing for sure that a storm was coming. She just wasn't sure what kind of storm it was or from which direction it was coming.

She called Carl and scheduled a meeting for ten o'clock. They had to talk, just the two of them.

They decided to meet outside and walk around the campus for a post-mortem on the prior day's weird meetings. A good sleep helped put things in proper perspective. Julie decided to bring along a transistor radio and play the Rushe Limpbaugh talk show so they could confuse any third parties who might be trying to listen in. They were paranoid for a reason; some of these government guys were real spooks and the guy from yesterday was at the top of their Creepy Guys list.

As Rushe blathered on, Carl and Julie walked among the

trees and ponds and spoke sotto voce about their new and super-weird assignment.

At first, they talked about the ethical, legal, and moral questions and rehashed some prior philosophical thinking, but they blew through this dialog fairly quickly. This was really just a conversational retread with a different product. In most ways, the issues they were now discussing were not that different from those accompanying their medical science projects and the general question about tinkering with Mother Nature's Master Code. It always boiled down to the same question and with the same answer: should we or shouldn't we tool around with the source code of life? If fortunate enough to have been placed in the position to decide, the answer was yes. Cementing their conclusion was the irrefutable understanding that if they didn't do the work, someone else would. Since they thought more highly of themselves than they did of other people who might pick up the mantle, they should do the work before someone else got the chance. Basically, they considered themselves less likely to fuck things up than anybody else. They were done with the preamble.

"The key here is to *not* think too hard about the who and the why, and keep our eyes on the what and the how," she shrugged, still feeling the aftershocks of yesterday's fear. Changing her tone, she added, "Remember tripping our brains out walking around the Mayan ruins, pondering the meaning of life, looking at the stars, accepting their place and ours in the great cosmos and the strangeness inherent in the mushrooms we picked off good old cowshit? Well, Carl, I think psilocybin might be part of the compound we need to build for the creepmeister."

Carl turned to look at her through narrowed eyes. "Go on."

"Psilocybin changed the way we saw each other, other people, our surroundings, our senses of trust and threat, and our abilities to perceive. It changed just about everything." She told him about her restless and fitful sleep and that Mexico and their psychedelic recreation had wafted in and out of her dreams. "So what do you think? This agent is, after all, about altering perception and that has everything to do with wavelengths, correct?"

"There is no doubt that we were picking up things, vibes, call them what you will, that we wouldn't have otherwise perceived," Carl agreed. "We picked up something or there was a filter to block out other wavelengths. Those mushrooms made things very different, not just at the moment, but forever."

"Oh, and by the way, I changed the name of the project to something a bit less melodramatic and stupid. It's now code-named Project 4.20," Julie said with a slight smile. "The numbers correspond to the positions of the first letters of the original code name. D is 4 and T is…"

"I got it, Julie," Carl cut her off in mid sentence. "Very cute and clever and apropos. I'm with you on this already. I had a similar thought while the creepster was lecturing to us yesterday. We need to position this in such a way that Paulo doesn't think we've been passing around joints like freshmen in a college dorm room."

"I can almost hear him saying something like, "Oh yeah, pass the bong over here, dude. I want to get as stupid as you two. Are you guys fucking nuts?"

"If we couch this in terms of super-sensitive perceptivity and couple it with something physiological, say the pineal gland's role, we might be able to sell him. There is also a role for gene analysis and sequencing. Those variables would capture his imagination and get him in a comfort zone. I don't want to create the impression that we're just rehashing the psychoactive drug experiments the CIA did in the fifties and sixties," Carl said. "I was up half the night thinking about this. I don't want to propose something that is too wild. I also don't want to propose something that is simply drug-based, particularly an illegal drug. The Feds are scared shitless this stuff might become popular again and it would be a public relations nightmare. We'd all be screwed."

"Very excellent, Garth," Julie said. "I'm with you so far."

"Right on, Wayne," Carl quickly replied. "We should consider the efficacy as both a positive or negative screen; catching or rejecting thought patterns based on wavelength type. This will also help get Paulo on board."

Julie and Carl continued their walk in silence for a few minutes. It was a beautiful morning and they were getting close to the sphere that Julie could see from her office window.

Carl started again, "We should research the possible roles that clairvoyance or telepathy might also play. There is certainly a lot of research done in this area. It's also particularly interesting that much of the research studied the importance of wavelengths as aids in extrasensory perception. It's logical to include these specific categories of ESP. Basically we are now talking about coupling ESP with LSD. We'll write it up so that it is a bit more obtuse, but that's the gist of it so far, plus the physiological stuff. The notion of essentially combining ESP with psilocybin or LSD is an ambitious idea. Who knows what might leap out of this Petri dish. You know the phrase, 'just like in tennis and in marriage, success has everything to do with selecting the right partner.' Maybe we're really on to something here, old buddy. On the surface it seems like a good marriage."

"Who are you calling old? Let's hope this marriage doesn't end up like Burton and Taylor," Julie said with a laugh. "Either of them."

"It could. We have some pretty volatile ingredients already, and this is just our first walk. I can see the headlines already, RE-SEARCHERS LOST IN PSYCHOCOSMIC FUGUE!"

They laughed together, their current situation infused with their history .

A minute or so later Carl spoke up again. "Remember rhythmo-phosphenic function?" Carl asked.

"Vaguely," Julie replied. "If I remember it's the action of alternating hearing and vision frequencies that belong to a broad category of sensory awareness. Not much really. Very little work had been done on it the last time I looked at it, but that was twenty or so years ago."

"That's right," Carl said. "There is a precise cerebral function associated with it. There has been some new research over the past ten years, enough to give it a new name. It's now a big enough deal to have earned an acronym—the 'RP,'—but it's still wide-open territory. We should have somebody review the recent literature and see if there's a reason to include this along with the other variables. I think they've been looking for an anatomical link."

"Will do," Julie said. "This has been a very good chat. Thanks, old buddy."

"Now who's being called old?"

Julie smiled and said, "I'm going to go back to my office and put fingers to keyboard and pass out a few assignments. I also need to do some reading myself, particularly in the area of psychotropics. I think I'll give the Chili King a ring."

"You mean Earp?" Carl asked with a smile. "That's a great idea! He probably knows more about psychotropics than anyone alive. Be careful how much you disclose. He's a cagey one. Tell him I said hello and that I look forward to his next chili party. I don't know what he does to those peppers he roasts, but that chili of his is the best I've ever had. Maybe that's what happens when you turn a botanist into a cook."

"Will do," Julie said. "I'll tell him I'm reviewing an NIH grant request to treat alcoholism with LSD. That should bring out the best in him."

"Tomorrow, same time and place?" Carl asked.

"Perfect. Thanks, Carl. See you then," Julie said.

Julie went back to her office, looked out at the sphere, and thought, *That was a great conversation. This is going to be really fun.* She then began typing at her blistering speed of 85 words per minute. She rarely made mistakes typing or even when she wrote with a pen and paper. Her ideas blossomed and flowed logically and flawlessly. Using a keyboard almost allowed her to keep up with her thoughts.

She then set up a meeting for an hour hence and invited three of her top researchers—Niconor, the nutty Uruguayan; Jimmy, the rock climber; and Suzie, the drummer. These were her go-to people. When she needed something done right and in a hurry, she called on one or all of these folks.

When they arrived at her office, they had each already read the one page summary that Julie had sent with her meeting request. They were already on board. Jimmy called in for the meeting. It was his vacation day, and he made the call from the side of a mountain. He was about 1500 feet up and 1700 feet short of the top when his phone buzzed. So, he just parked himself on the face of the cliff, had lunch reading the one-pager, and waited for the meeting.

When the meeting started, Julie said, "Hi everybody. Thanks for coming on such short notice. Jimmy thanks for calling in on your vacation day. What are you doing?"

"Thanks for asking, Julie. Not much really, just hanging around,"

Jimmy said. "Check your e-mail. I just sent you a picture."

Julie opened the photo on her large projection screen and ex-claimed, "Jimmy, you are out of your mind, thanks for sharing, but no more distractions. We have a lot of work to do and we need to get started right away. You've got the history and the lat-est on ESP. Look specifically for any genetics-related work and also for anatomical- or physiological-related work. Niconor, look into RPF, history, and the ten most recent and ten most relevant studies. Our interest is most likely related more to reception and perception, but I would not overlook production or generation.

"Suzie, you've got the latest in psychobiology and LSD. Just don't take any of this stuff until the project's over. I need you focused," Julie said with a chuckle. She glanced at her Breitling Windrider Cockpit timepiece and authoritatively said, "So, it's 1:45. Let's meet at 9:30 tonight and see what we've learned. Jim-my, since you're literally on the hook, I'll let you off the hook until tomorrow. While we're all together, let's also plan on another ses-sion at six p.m. tomorrow. Five minutes each, round robin. Any questions? Okay, thanks everybody. See you later," she concluded.

That's good, Julie thought. *I'll have the equivalent of fifty hours of top-notch research in seven hours. These guys are really fast.*

Carl took a different approach and followed a hunch on radio waves. He was doing his own research.

Julie then picked up the phone and called the Chili King.

"Wyatt, Julie Perthuis. How are you?" Julie asked in a friendly but professional voice.

"Well, I'll be. To what do I owe the pleasure of a call from the SS? We haven't talked in a year or so. I am exhilarated to be hearing the voice of the world's sexiest scientist. You are so beau-tiful you've made an absolutely indelible mark in my memory. You know I often think about you? Are you still cavorting with that neo-con physician? How about you dump him and you and I ride off into the sunset?"

"Wyatt, you are as charming as ever. Thank you. I do like flattery, even if it's coming from you. You spew out some of the best bullshit I've ever heard, and so effortlessly. So consistently. And yes, Clark and I are still cavorting and our kids are doing fine. Everything good on your end?" Julie inquired.

"Yeah, I guess," Earp replied with a hint of weariness. "Nothing to complain about. Still crawling around looking for flora and fungi."

"Still selling naming rights?" Julie questioned. "That's the cleverest fundraising gimmick I've ever heard of."

"Absolutely," Earp said. "Except now, I only close the deals while wearing high heels and no underwear. I want to really feel like a whore. I'm guessing that's why you've called, you want to name something after Clark."

"Very funny!" Julie exclaimed. "It's no wonder you are such a hit with the philanthropy crowd. Those blue-haired women must be clamoring over you. I'm sorry to tell you that Dr. Conservative doesn't get a plant named after him. I'm calling because I need to pick your brain if I can."

"Sure, Julie, anything for you," Earp replied sincerely. "And in your case I do mean that literally."

"Thank you," she said. "I've been asked to review an NIH grant involving hallucinogens and their potential for treating alcoholism. I was hoping you would shoot over some links on history and research on psychotropics; types, morphology, potencies, organic, manufactured, side effects, sources, you know the drill, as much as you can come up with on short notice."

"If they're trying to see if hallucinogens cure alcoholism, tell them to just send the frickin' money directly to me. I've tried them all and I still drink like there's no tomorrow," Earp snorted. "How soon do you want this stuff?"

"As soon as possible. I was called in as a replacement for another reviewer and I'd like to wrap it up and get back to my own business."

"Okay, I'll see what I can come up with."

"Great, Wyatt. I really appreciate it. Carl said to say hello and to ask you about the next chili fiesta," Julie said.

"I'll let him know. Say hello. I'll get back to you," Earp said and hung up.

Julie thought, *That's one peculiar man. I hope if we start reading minds I don't go into his. It seems like a very complicated and chronically conflicted place.*

Earp kicked back in his chair, put his feet on his desk, twirled his moustache and thought, *NIH my ass. What the fuck are those guys up to now? Knowing them, it could be anything.*

Chapter Thirteen

W hen Julie and Carl met the next day after having done a little homework, they were surprised that their developing hypotheses dovetailed with some of the theories promoted by a Dr. Francis Lefebre, a Parisian physician and researcher, who made many discoveries in cerebral physiology during the 1960s. These discoveries helped explain, or at least frame, the mechanisms of clairvoyance. His research was based on the systematic use of the phosphenes. Phosphenes are the subjective sensations of light. These sensations, however, are not directly provoked by light stimulating the retina. Phosphenes can be obtained by *focusing on sources* of light for short periods of time.

Part of Carl's hypothesis also brought with it the theories of Houck. Jack Houck earned his MS degree in Aeronautical and Astronautical Engineering from the University of Michigan. He retired after forty-two years with Boeing as a systems engineer. In his spare time, though, he researched the paranormal. He first became interested in this field in the 1970s when he read an article reporting that the CIA trained remote viewers to psychically spy on the Russians during the Cold War. This idea was actually very similar to what project 4.20 was about.

Houck also became fascinated with psychokinesis (PK) or mind over matter. According to varying reports, he taught over 20,000 people how to bend spoons with their minds through seminars on psychic healing. He had as many supporters as he had detractors, but he did make a name for himself and provided some framework for the so-called field of PK. His underlying theory made sense. Clear the mind of distracting noise and therefore enable it to concentrate and focus its resources, its energy, on or toward a specific target. By doing this, the mind's psychic and electrical energy could be pointed at a spoon and converted into force.

Houck's research in PK and remote viewing was fascinating, but what really caught Carl's attention was a discovery he made about psychics. Houck collected the EEGs of psychics, yogis, shamans, and psychic healers and analyzed their data. He observed that they all had a specific brain frequency in common: 7.83 Hz. That, by itself, was an eye-popping conclusion. But Houck then wondered what would happen if he could stimulate this frequency in a non-psychic person. Would that person become hyper-sensitive?

To find the answer, Houck devised a clever method to test his theory using extremely low frequency (ELF) wavelengths, specifically 7.83 Hz of sound. Since ELFs are too low for the human ear to sense them, Houck coupled the ELF with an audible frequency and then placed headphones on non-psychics. After about twenty minutes, fifty percent of the test subjects had an out-of-body experience. Houck also noted that this same 7.83 Hz is attained naturally during REM sleep, and when someone is in a meditative yogic state. This could explain why some people have premonitions or ghostly encounters while dreaming, and why some psychics need to be in a self-hypnotic trance state to conduct readings or communicate with the dead. Perhaps this frequency trait is genetic, explaining why psychic ability is passed from generation to generation.

But why 7.83 Hz? What makes this frequency so special and why does the human brain react the way it does when exposed to it? Houck theorized that it involved Mother Nature. He believed that the space or atmosphere between the earth's surface and the ionosphere, about thirty miles above the earth's surface, oscillated at this same magnetic frequency. Quite astonishingly, Houck was correct.

Houck believed that all time/space information is stored within this "atmospheric computer" surrounding the earth. The way to access this information was to tune into the 7.83 Hz frequency. It apparently needed an amplifier, pre-amp, antenna, or something, but Hauck never got that far. The notion is a common thought among musicians and songwriters. Most composers refer to their writing more as discovering songs rather than truly creating them. Some great players actually used the term antenna to refer to their ability to play great improvisations, capture great music, or *tap in*. This theorizing was also very Jungian and helped put some substance behind Jung's theories on the collective unconscious.

Houck theorized that when the brain's frequency is synced up with the earth's frequency at 7.83 Hz, an individual may have access to all the information of all time and space. Houck also believed that when the human mind goes beyond the anatomical or physical brain, it can act as a receiver or transmitter inside the "super computer of all information of all existence," not just that of our planet and that humans could see and hear the past, present, and future in all places and planes of existence. Houck believed this frequency was the key, a universal user ID and password, into the all-knowing of all things in the universe.

Today this is known as the Schumann Resonance. This global electromagnetic resonance phenomenon is named after physicist Winfried Otto Schumann who predicted it mathematically in 1952. Schumann Resonances occur because the space between the surface of the Earth and the conductive ionosphere behaves as a closed waveguide. The limited dimensions of the Earth cause this waveguide to act as a resonant cavity for all types of electromagnetic wavelengths. In the normal mode descriptions of Schumann Resonances, the fundamental mode is referred to as a standing wave, in this so-called resonant cavity. This lowest-frequency (and highest-intensity) mode of the Schumann Resonance occurs at 7.83 Hz.

Carl saw this as a godsend discovery, literally. He felt as Leonardo must have felt when he realized the significance of pi. Or when Shirley Tilghman realized she had the *whole* answer when her colleague unwittingly solved the other half of her problem by describing his own problem. For each of them, and for the many others who have made powerful insights into the "natural workings," for at least a moment, they knew something really valuable and significant that *no one else knew.* This profound realization came along with feelings of awe, power, fear, and respect. When Carl absorbed the importance of what he realized, he was overwhelmed, fell back in his chair and let out a huge holy-fuck sigh. *It's just like a fucking remote or garage door opener,* he thought. *We just don't know where the TV is yet.* Carl had just discovered half the answer to a method that would change everything from communication and travel to learning and medicine. Instead of just reading minds, he now believed he could change them. *Let's get a transducer, pump the voltage, and start shooting. We're almost ready to power up the hovercraft.*

Prior to Houck's research, the first documented observation of global electromagnetic resonance was at the Colorado Springs laboratory of Nikola Tesla in 1899. This observation led to certain peculiar conclusions about the electrical properties of the earth, and which made the basis for his scheme for wireless energy transmission. Although some of the most important mathematical tools for dealing with spherical waveguides were developed in the early 1900s, it was Schumann who first studied the theoretical aspects of the global resonances of the earth's ionosphere and the waveguide system.

Researching radio waves, Tesla, and Marconi led Carl to Houck and in turn to Schumann's Resonance. Tesla researched ways to transmit power and energy wirelessly over long distances. He transmitted extremely low frequencies through the ground as well as between the Earth's surface and the Kennelly-Heaviside layer. He received patents on wireless transceivers that developed standing waves by this method. In his experiments, he made mathematical calculations and computations based on his experiments and discovered also, that the resonant frequency of the Earth was approximately 8 Hz. In the 1950s, researchers confirmed that the resonant frequency of the Earth's ionospheric cavity was in this range.

From the very beginning of Schumann Resonance studies, it was known that they could be used to monitor lightning. At any given time, there are about 2,000 thunderstorms around the globe, producing approximately 50 lightning events each second of every day. It seemed somehow logical that these naturally occurring ELF's were initiated by lightning. Lightning discharges are considered to be the primary natural energy source of Schumann Resonances. Lightning makes electrons in the atmosphere oscillate. Lightning channels behave like huge power discharges that radiate electromagnetic energy. These signals are very weak at large distances from the lightning source, but the earth–ionosphere waveguide behaves like a resonator and amplifies the spectral signals from lightning at the resonance frequencies. Based on the connection between lightning and the earth's climate, Schumann Resonances have been used to monitor global temperature variations and variations of water vapor in the upper troposphere. It has been speculated that extraterrestrial lightning, the lightning on other planets, may also be detected and measured by using Schumann Resonances. Recently, Schumann Resonances have been linked to transient luminous events including sprites, jets, elves and other upper-atmospheric lightning. A new field of interest using Schumann resonances is related to short-term earthquake prediction.

Today Schumann Resonances are recorded at many research stations around the world. Although they are extensively used in research and studied in and of themselves, they are still considered enigmas.

The more Carl thought about all of this, the more sense it made. It was just too Jungian. It was just too logical. They had a few new ingredients to add to the recipes on ESP. Carl knew he was on to something. He needed a new power source or a new biological partner to enable powerful reliable use. This would now become part of the theories he and Julie were building and the hook of all hooks to bring Paulo into their tent.

The next morning when Carl and Julie took their walk, Julie couldn't help but noticing that Carl looked both tired and wired. He seemed animated. Carl started talking first.

"I was up all night," Carl said with enthusiasm. "I stumbled into the work of Jack Houck who did very thoughtful research on the sound frequency of 7.83 Hz."

"Oh, the Schumann Resonance?"

"Precisely," Carl responded, disappointed that he wasn't bringing Julie a tasty new intellectual morsel. "You came across it also?"

"Yep," Julie said. "Jimmy and Niconor each mentioned it in their initial findings last night. How do you want to use it in our hypothesis?"

"I want to bombard organic psychotropics, specifically psilocybin, with extreme doses of 7.83 Hz," Carl said. "If my theory is correct, this peak wavelength is like the garage door opener to the universe. When Huxley wrote *The Doors to Perception*, I don't think he had this giant door in mind. If I'm correct, we will not only be able to read minds, we will be able to alter thought patterns at the individual or group level."

"Yikes!" Julie remarked. "Did I hear someone say fascism? Aren't we going beyond our charter with this? We're supposed to stick to better sensing, not thought management or thought control?"

Carl responded with an admonishing tone, "Hey, we both know the nature of research. You know exactly where you are when you start and have no idea where you will be when it's over. It's the serendipitous outcome that makes otherwise boring lab work so attractive. We stumble around in the Skinner Box and every once in a while bump in to the magic bar that dumps out all the money and triggers the casino lights and bells. I think this "mother bar" is in the box, I'm just not sure where yet."

"Carl, you never cease to amaze me. This does make sense. I'll change my draft to reflect this variable and adjust my materials and equipment requisition list to include low frequency sound wave generators and some transducers to boost the voltage. I should have the hypotheses ironed out by tonight and the requisition list done as well. I am including mature psilocybin fungi, dry spores, various growing media, and a very hard-to-find substance called schlorocia. This last item is very obscure. We'll see how well Mike does with this one," Julie concluded.

Schlorocia was a biotype and the active agent in psilocybin. It was a sort of "starter yeast" for this particular variety of psychoactive mushroom. The important or "active part" of the psilocybin mushroom—or any type of mushroom for that matter—remains phenotypic and retains its cell integrity regardless of its size or form, whether it is in the stage of a spore or whether it has fruited and shown itself. The mushroom that presents itself, regardless of its type, is basically there to hold water and provide a mechanism for reproduction.

Mushrooms produce spores that spread and grow into new fungi. Despite being called fruiting, the mushroom does not actually produce fruit, but produces spores that reside under the cap on the gills of the mushroom. The visible part of the mushroom is only a small part of the entire fungus. Long threadlike strands called mycelia spread out beneath the soil or host medium. The earth is literally covered with them; there are thousands of varieties of fungi and they are everywhere, even if they are not visible to the eye. As these strands grow, they absorb nutrients and water, providing energy for growth. Eventually, the mushroom manifests itself, it is thought, for the sole purpose of spreading its spores. Most fungi are obligate saprophytic feeders. They are designed to eat only dead things. They are the earth's recyclers. Without them we would choke and drown in our own waste in a matter of a decade or so.

Some psilocybin mushrooms use cow patties in specific climates as their hosts. After rain, the fungus manifests itself in the form of a mushroom and is either consumed or it dries out, cast-

---

ing its spores into the wind. The digestion of cow waste is very important, and not without its irony. It is with this ugly, smelly bovine turd that a special peek into the vastness of the universe is provided through a beautiful symbiotic union.

"Add some samples of the pineal gland," Carl suggested. "I want to get the genomics guys to pick this apart and see what we find. I have a feeling this might be part of my antennae theory."

Julie said, "I'm going to have Paulo make the first call to T Mike. I'll sit in on it, but I want Paulo to be all in on this."

"Agreed," Carl said. "I'm going to go take a nap for an hour or so, I'm wiped out."

"Pleasant dreams," Julie joked. "Call when you want to talk, you know where I'll be."

Chapter Fourteen

J ulie watched as Paulo re-read Julie's one-page project plan summary. They were in the sitting area of Paulo's glass-walled office, comfortably seated in a pair of Eames chairs covered in a wonderfully soft, dark-brown suede. The summary included the main hypotheses, time lines, and supplies, where available. She could see Paulo's intense focus and little hints of skepticism or elevated interest as he raised his eyebrows or curved his lips in a slight smile.

Paulo put the paper on his lap and closed his eyes for almost a minute before looking up at Julie. "At first, I thought that you and Carl must have been drinking or at least not thinking clearly. This is a rather complex and ambitious body of thought. You intend to use psychotropic botanicals, link them to the anatomy and physiology of paranormal thinking, sequence the related genes in the pineal gland, plug in genes from schlorocia and serotonin, and then use Schumann's Resonance as some kind of delivery medium catalyst or magnifier. Is that a fair summary?" Paulo questioned.

"That's the gist of it, yes," Julie replied in a confident but dis-passionate tone.

"Well, as I said, upon my first reading, I though you two had left the reservation, but after my third reading, I think you might be on to something. The notion that we may be able to actually adjust or alter thought patterns and additionally, convert and power-up psychic energy, goes quite beyond our assignment from Mr. Reynolds. That said, it is the Holy Grail. Let's do two things. First let's agree that the over-and-above work—that is, the thought control and enhanced psychic energy uses pieces of this work—stays in-house. We'll keep that to ourselves. I'm not going to give that away for twenty-five million dollars. Twenty-five billion, maybe, and that's a big maybe. So, rewrite your summary and research methodologies and so forth to reflect the more narrow of the research efforts—Mike's. We'll cover the other items concurrently. Schedule the trials so that the results will be coterminous. Second, let's get Mike on the phone. I agree with your recommendation that I initiate and lead this first call. He'll want to know, and hear in my voice, that I'm on board with more than just the fear that he'd turn the dogs loose on us."

"One more thing before we call Mike. From an experimental design point of view, I don't need to tell you that you have a lot of moving parts and too many independent variables," Paulo remarked. "You've simply introduced more risk and uncertainty and less control than you would generally want. But, I have full trust in your research capabilities and you've put together a good team. I like Suzie, Niconor, and Jimmy the wacky rock climber. Thanks for sending me his meeting participation photo. That was pretty funny. We need guys like him. Good hire," Paulo concluded.

With that, Paulo hit the speaker button on the table phone and pressed number four on the keypad. This was now the speed dial to Mike's cell phone.

"Good morning, Paulo," Mike said. "How are you this morning?"

"We're great. It's a beautiful day here and I am here with Julie. I want to update you on our progress and send you a requisition list," Paulo said. "Decrypt it using the protocols we discussed. Along with the bill of materials I'm including a one-page summary of the plan, key hypotheses, and time lines. You should have it in a couple of hours. I don't intend to get into any of the details over the phone, but I have to say I am now very excited about the prospects of this research. As you remember, I was skeptical when we met a few days ago, but Julie, Carl, and their teams have developed a plan that has far exceeded my expectations. It is bold, ambitious, and offers excellent promise. Their work has been energizing," Paulo trumpeted.

"I am not the slightest bit surprised and expected nothing less. That is why I chose you for this. There is no one better," Mike replied. "I'll review your summary and get whatever it is you're requesting in the works this afternoon. Unless there is something very unusual on your list, expect a delivery tomorrow. Let me emphasize that I have no interest or intent in participating in the management or direction of this project beyond what I've already told you. I do, however, want to kept abreast of its progress each week as we agreed."

"That's right Mike. I expect our Friday calls to last no more than five to ten minutes," replied Julie.

"That's perfect. Thanks for the call and I'll look forward to your written communication," Mike said.

Paulo had a solid, working knowledge of organic chemistry. His original field was botany. Years before, he had been intrigued by the comprehensive work done by Schultes and Hoffman on the botany and chemistry of hallucinogenic plants, so he knew there was a great deal of untilled soil to be explored.

Paulo had looked into Schumann's Resonance himself, but no

one really knew much about it beyond its description. Meteorologists and astronomers knew what it was, but its purpose was very much a mystery. It was kind of like the Bose-Einstein Condensate—physicists know of it, experiment with it, but no one's quite sure why it's here and what purpose it might serve.

Paulo sat at his large desk and looked out at the well-groomed corporate campus of HugMap. His desk was a six by four foot vein-cut slab of Verde Issorie. The highly polished green marble surface had unfinished edges and was supported by found industrial objects. Its base was abstract expressionism in steel. The top was thousands of years old. It was a functional metaphor for the nature of their work; the old and the new, the use and reuse of things found.

Hugmap's campus had been designed to encourage open thought and passionate intellectual discourse. To help stimulate good and regular thinking, all of Hugmap's employees were required to complete a reading list consisting of the great Greek, Chinese, Japanese, European, American, and Indian philosophers. Each year Paulo added a few more titles based on input from employees.

This project, more than others, put big questions on the table. Much of their work pushed ethical and moral boundaries, but this project had pushed them way past the Rubicon.

As he gazed at Henry Moore's "Nuclear Energy," a bronze sculpture depicting the beginning of the Nuclear Age, he thought about the volatile mix of variables they were toying with and the inherent unpredictability of experimentation. He'd purchased this sculpture from the Regenstein Library a year ago as a reminder to himself—and to his employees, investors, clients, and board—about the Law of Unintended Consequences. Regardless of the discipline and the rigor they built into their practices and processes, unanticipated results were always part of the outcome. In this project, he had a strong and odd feeling that these unanticipated outcomes would be significant.

As Paulo free-associated about their project, some of the research on light that he had read years ago came to mind. He had a fleeting thought that some very narrow peak wavelength of light might end up being part of their solution. Ultraviolet light had been associated with this area of research for years. He also thought about the use of psychotropics. Research had been dormant for nearly five decades, ever since the highly negative press they received in the 60s and 70s. As good as the intentions of the hippies and flower children might have been, their association with psychotropics killed research for nearly five decades. Paulo thought how pleased he was to have such open-minded, if not prescient, researchers on his staff.

Energized by the unexpected direction his team had developed, he stood up, walked close to his office window, and looked out over the magnificent grounds. He felt grand and important. *This could be so much bigger than the Bellihurton project. This could actually be the most significant discovery in history. It has the potential to change the world as we've known it. This could also be my ticket into the history books. I'd be in the same group as Archimedes, Pasteur, Marie Curie, Fermi, and Einstein. Wowwie wow wow wow!*

With this as his psychological and emotional backdrop, Paulo decided to take a walk around campus and chat with his employees. His attitude would not get more inspiring than it was at the moment.

PART TWO

Chapter Fifteen

The basic hypothesis that Julie and Carl had come up with was that ESP, coupled with a still-to-be-determined psychotropic chemical compound, would produce hypersensitive perceptual abilities. Specific gene sequences—those associated with extrasensory perception, clairvoyance, telepathy, and telekinesis—would be mapped. In parallel, the sequences of various psychotropic compounds would be detailed. With these two components as tools or ingredients, a new product, or agent, would be created.

Clairvoyance, the so-called art of seeing things that are beyond the five human senses, was the specific target of their experimental design. Sometimes referred to as the sixth sense, it is often described by the classic example wherein a person sits in one room and looks at pictures or numbers on cards while another person, sitting in a separate room, describes the numbers or pictures the person with those cards sees. Telepathy, on the other hand, is simply the "science" of reading someone else's mind from afar. Their work would fall somewhere between these two poorly understood psychic phenomena. Their experimental goal was to have a little of each ability in their final product.

Julie sat back in her olive-colored Dania, Fulkrum desk chair, nibbled on a handful of pitted dates and roasted cashews and pondered the ambitious research she and Carl were about to undertake. *Damn comfy chair. I hope our designs work out as well.* They were going to map the 600 or so genes in the pineal gland and also those in serotonin. Many researchers who had studied the paranormal believed the physiology of extrasensory experiences could be found in the pineal gland. Julie wondered why the pineal was anatomically and genetically similar to the make-up of the human eye. *Was this some sort of clue that the grand wizard dropped in the mix just for laughs and then tucked it into the center of the brain's anterior region just to make things difficult? Was this thing really some kind of "third eye," as some believed?*

The gene concentration in the pineal is greater than in any other tissue in the human body. Many in the medical community theorized that the gland plays a much broader role in human health, behavior, and perception than anyone had ever imagined. The gland is synchronized to a 24-hour time period and actively participates in regulating our sleep-wake cycles. Neuroendocrinologists involved in studying it have concluded there is long way to go before we fully understand the role of this peculiar part of the human body. The pineal used to be a comparatively large part of the human brain and was once about the size of a large lime. Over time, it has shrunk to about the size of a pea. It is considered by some to be nothing more than an anatomical remnant; the glandular equivalent of the appendix. Others believe it has great significance and has shrunk because humans either forgot how, or lost the ability, to use it thousands of years ago.

Concurrent with this mapping, Julie and her team would delve deeply into psychopharmacology. This was the area Julie found the most interesting among the many factors they were including in their designs. Psilocybin and a range of other psychotropic or psychomimetic plants would also be mapped. Their genomes would be decoded and sequenced. Then, using gene splicing, supercomputing, and the nifty Swith-Waterman algorithm (SWA), they would try to bind or blend the various components into a structure that allowed super-sensitive perception on demand. The delivery mechanism had not yet been given any thought. They knew serotonin would play a role, as it was the neurotransmitter most closely related with the chemistry and physiology they were studying.

Julie was certain her instinct for including the 'shroom as part of a potential solution was correct. She was delighted when a moment later she saw an e-mail from Earp pop up on her screen. *Great! This should make our lives, particularly mine, much easier. Earp probably just saved me weeks of work.*

The e-mail's subject line was "Primer on Psychopharmacology." When Julie clicked it open, the note read,

> *Dr. Perthuis,*
>
> *Please find the attached. This brief summary may provide you with more questions than answers, but it will give you useful general background. The links to some current work should allow you to follow your nose as it dictates. I've opined here and there, but for the most part just kept to the facts. I sincerely hope you find this reading as stimulating as I did when compiling it for you. As accidental as your involvement might be with the review you mentioned, I have little doubt the attached will be but a first step for you in a field I have found intellectually challenging and fulfilling for decades. As always, it was delightful speaking with you and I do hope to see you soon.*
>
> *With warm regards, Earp*

Julie clicked open the attached document, renamed it and saved it in the 4.20 file on HGMP's network, copied it to a flash drive and then tossed the drive back in to her purse. She was fanatical about backing up her systems and work content. She, like everybody else who was born into the generation where personal computers were new products, had learned the hard way about not backing up. Julie lost an entire weekend once because she got so lost in thought she forgot to back up. Then her system crashed and thirty hours of VisiCalc®-based work evaporated like ether, a mistake never to be repeated.

Earp's document was titled "A Primer on Psychopharmacology."

> The first thing to keep in mind when entering the field of psychopharmacology is that all known hallucinogenic "plants" are of vegetal origin. This conclusion, although evangelistic-minded mycologists would vehemently disagree, takes the research directly to the field of botany. Mycological purists, the students of fungi per se, consider their field truly distinct from the green plant kingdom, or those organisms relying exclusively on photosynthesis for life support. Mycologists believe, and with a body of solid and convincing data to support them, that fungi should not just have their own species, but they should specifically not be subsumed under the umbrella of botanical life. These naturally occurring fungal life forms, some with hallucinogenic properties, have existed for hundreds of millions of years before Homo Sapiens emerged. They are morphologically distinct from green plants.
>
> Since formal work in this area is really just beginning, it is generally accepted that the scientific and medical communities have not even begun to scratch

the surface of the fungi's purpose or to grasp the utility they may have to offer. One thing remains common among all those that have become empirically familiar with the perception-enhancing experiences produced by ingesting psychoactive fungi is that the experience cannot be fully communicated with language. The words *hallucinogenic, psychedelic, psychomimetics, narcotic, and mind-enhancing* do not effectively capture the fundamental and transcendental nature of the experiences they produce.

Here are a few facts for you, Julie.

Biologists estimate the number of species on earth to be somewhere between 3 million and 100 million.

Recent studies estimate that Earth has almost 8.8 million species, but that only a fraction of these species has been discovered. Of these species, 6.5 million would be on land and 2.2 million in the ocean, give or take. Estimates suggest that animals make up the largest group with 7.8 million species, followed by fungi with 611,000 and plants with about 300,000 species. So far, only 1.9 million of the 8.8 species have been discovered. As I am sure you will agree, we are just beginning to recognize the remarkable variety of life forms living on our planet. Viewed through the lens of wavelength perception, (where I presume you will be headed as you delve more deeply into this field), it is both exciting and unsettling how little we understand.

As to the area of psychoactive plants and fungi, there are about 120 species of hallucinogenic plants out of a combined plant and fungus population of approximately 900,000 species, or roughly one out of 7,500 species. The precise number of plant species may never be accurately determined and certainly never complete. New species are discovered each year and old species die. As you noted during our phone conversation, this is a recurring opportunity for me to maintain my lofty big-money-man status.

Making things all the more curiouser and curiouser, the Western world has an unexplained concentration of the planet's hallucinogenic plants, particularly the fungi. There are hallucinogenic plants and fungi in both hemispheres that are not all used as psychotropics. Plants with hallucinogenic properties also occur in most of the earth's climates. For inexplicable reasons, however, most of these plants with psychotropic effects found their most hospitable environments in the Western hemisphere, and specifically in Central and South America.

Adding to this curiosity is that psychotropic plants, and fungi in specific, are conspicuously absent from what anthropologists and archaeologists consider to be the birthplace of civilization, where the Tigris and the Euphrates meet. Some speculate that the white man had to escape his surroundings and make the dangerous journey to the New World to discover these strange life forms that offer a portal into the vast and inexplicable universe.

Julie, this is useful history and may be a place to begin branching out into other areas. Louis Lewin, the author of *Phantastica*,[1] grouped psychoactive plants into five categories; ecitania, enebriantia, hypnotica, euphorica, and phantastica. Lewin's interests were in this last category, the phantastica, the plants that produced so-called hallucinations. "Hallucinogens, or psychomimetics, in effect, are plants or chemical agents, which in non-toxic doses produce, together or alone, changes in perception, thought, and mood, without causing major disturbances to the autonomic nervous system. Significantly, addiction is unknown with these drugs," *The Botany and Chemistry of Hallucinogenic Plants*, by Drs. Schultes and Hofmann.[2]

This subject area gets even stranger. Oddly, many active psychotropic agents are not processed by the kidney and remain active and potent after having been evacuated out of the body. Consequently, the drinking of urine as part of religious rituals involving hallucinogens is not an uncommon practice among members of primitive tribes. "One of the world's earliest known religions was the cult of Soma, practiced by the Indo-Europeans of Central Asia. According to its sacred text, the Rig Veda, Soma was an intoxicant with the powers of a god. People worshiped the drug itself. Ethnobotanists now think this plant was *Amamita muscaria*, the mushroom sometimes called fly agaric. They used it as a path to divine knowledge."[3]

In 1932, a researcher by the name of Raoul Mourgue[4] reviewed, as far as he could tell, all of the available literature on hallucinogenic plants. He reviewed approximately 7,000 publications. He concluded that there was not an adequate basis to *even build a theory as to the purpose and existence of hallucinogenic mushrooms!*

Mourgue was a brilliant man, tireless researcher and expansive thinker. For him to have thrown in the towel on building a theoretical platform is worth noting.

This field you are about to study, or more accurately, this area of interest, has languished for decades. It has been diluted and blended into ethnology, ethno-anthropology, ethno-deism, the occult, cultural theism, and other areas of obscure interest. Importantly, there was no money to be made, or so everyone thought.

Then, came along April 16, 1942 and the industry of psychopharmacology was cast into the spotlight with all mixed reactions that came along with Marylyn Monroe singing Happy Birthday, Mr. President. Albert Hofmann, PhD and Nobel Prize winner in the field of applied chemistry discovered lysergic acid diethylamide. Dr. Hofmann synthesized the active compounds found in psilocybin and produced LSD. Since his discovery and original papers, more than 20,000 publications have been written on the subject. The scientific disciplines of ethnomycology and psychomycology were created. The fields of pharmacology, psychiatry, and psychotherapy were forever changed.

Once LSD hit the streets, social life as everyone knew it was changed forever. There was a period of time extending into the late 1960s when LSD was legal. It was possible to call Sandoz Laboratories, Inc. in Switzerland and simply place an order for pure lysergic acid diethylamide. It was easy to order 200 millilitres of the substance and in a few days receive the chemical in 20-milliliter ampoules, fully sealed vials of chemically pure LSD. This was a remarkable period of time. The drug had great promise in the field of psychiatry, particularly for treating depression, and yes, even alcoholism. The drug irrevocably altered one's perception of the world and one's place in it.

This newly synthesized psycholubricant significantly altered perception due in part to its ability to increase or accelerate the uptake and transmission rates of excitatory neurotransmitters. The brain simply took in much more information and processed it more rapidly than without the chemical. People reported that they could smell colors and see odors. With the current understanding that physiology is largely wavelength sensitive, these findings which seemed without foundation fifty years ago, now have much more intuitive appeal and scientific support based on research done over the past few decades.

Hofmann's discoveries surrounding the chemical similarities between human serotonin and the active ingredient in psilocybin had and continue to have wide-ranging implications. The general importance of serotonin led to the foundation of the current pharmaceutical industry's product successes and boundless financial strength. Were it not for serotonin, we would not have the Prozac Generation, the generation that generates $250 billion in annual global sales. This commercial success is all tied, one-way or another, to serotonin and in turn to Dr. Albert Hofmann.

Julie, little did Dr. Hoffmann know that he really *did* turn the world around, but with serotonin, not LSD, as Hoffmann had expected.

No one explains serotonin better then James South.[5] "Serotonin is one of the ten or so major brain neurotransmitters; there are perhaps 100 minor neurotransmitters. Neurotransmitters are what the biochemical nerve cells use to 'talk' to each other. There are an estimated 100 billion neurons in the human brain, and each neuron may connect to thousands of other neurons. Yet these interconnecting neurons do not quite touch each other, there is a microscopic gap between them called the 'synaptic gap.' As a burst of electric current travels down the length of a neuron, it releases a packet of neurotransmitter molecules that are stored at the edge of the synaptic gap. These neurotransmitters then diffuse or jump across the synaptic gap and plug themselves into the receptor sites of the next neuron, like tiny keys fitting into locks. When a sufficient number of molecules have plugged into the corresponding receptors of the next neuron, this neuron then discharges a burst of electricity down its cell membrane surface, repeating the process with neurons to which it connects. Thus, neurons use electricity to propagate a signal down the length of their own cell structure, but use chemical neurotransmitter molecules to signal other neurons. When there are inadequate numbers of neurotransmitters to activate other neurons, various brain circuits become under or overactive due to lack of communication between nerve cells.

Studies with humans and animals have shown that serotonin nerve circuits promote feelings of well-being, calm, personal security, relaxation, confidence and concentration. Serotonin neural circuits also help counterbalance the tendency of brain dopamine and noradrenalin (two other major neurotransmitters) to encourage over-arousal, fear, anger, tension, aggression, violence, obsessive-compulsive actions, overeating, anxiety and sleep disturbances. Unfortunately, neuroscience has also discovered that many people suffer from various degrees of brain serotonin deficiency."

Julie, I hope this helps you and your colleagues. I know I've rambled on a bit longer than I might have otherwise, but for you, I just couldn't help myself.

Earp

Julie stood up from her chair and began pacing around her office. *Wow,* she thought, *what a wacky dude and how brilliant! He just saved me a boatload of work. That was a fantastic read. Now I know for sure I'm on the right track.*

Chapter Sixteen

After a week, Julie had given her small team well-structured, clear assignments. All of the materials they needed were at hand. They had created mini-ecosystems where they could grow fresh psilocybin, its variants, and a number of other psychotropic plants. Once grown, they were teased apart and the psychoactive agents were extracted and sent off for sequencing. They compared their findings on psilocybin morphology to that of schlorocia and found minor differences between the two. Those differences were concentration levels of the active mycelia and the wider range of acceptable growing media. The schlorocia were much smaller, much more potent, and reproduced much more easily than the larger fungal form of psilocybin. The schlorocia were also not as selective in choosing their host medium needed for reproduction.

Concurrent with this, they sequenced serotonin and the genes residing in the pineal gland. In one of the microenvironments, the fungi, some of which were now hybrids, were now reproducing on their own. This was an unanticipated and significant outcome. Special care had to be taken to ensure the specimens were well isolated and that they were not contaminated in any way.

In some of the experimental cells, the researchers were bombarding the fungi with 7.83 Hz before, during, and after germination. Julie's research team wasn't exactly sure what results they might get, but the basic null hypothesis was in place. That is, there would be no differences among any of the fungal groups.

They had a large number of experimental variables to control and examine, in order to determine if Schumann's Resonance would change anything. Much to their surprise, the psilocybin mushroom, schlorocia, and all of the hybrids grew faster in the 7.83 Hz environment. Consequently, this area began to get much more attention and study.

Considering the scope of their project and its secrecy, HGMP had surprisingly not instituted any additional advanced security protocols. Everyone simply needed to badge in and out of the building. All of the project's team members had the company's highest security clearances and were able to come and go with relative ease. Most of the team members wore white lab coats and had their badges clipped to their pockets or the lapels. When employees went home, they put their lab coat in their offices, grabbed their badge and buzzed out. It was a great security system because it kept a perfect digital record of who went where and when.

The bioengineering laboratory was well equipped. There were five island workstations, each with four sinks supporting various fields of application. The countertops on the islands and the wall-attached work surfaces were solid cast, monolithic Duratop epoxy resin, molded and oven-cured as solid, uniformly constructed surfaces, each with a smooth, nonspecular finish.

The lab also had wonderful equipment including drying ovens with forced convection for all standard drying and tempering tasks as well as sterilizing glassware. These units were microprocessor controlled with temperature readings in degrees centigrade. They each had exhaust ducts at the rear of the units with manually adjustable slides. The stainless steel interiors were equipped with two chrome-plated shelves. There were many sets of five borosilicate glass Erlenmeyer flasks and beakers, scales, round-bottom distilling kits, high-speed refrigerated micro-centrifuges, clinical microscopes, and fluorescence microscopes. They used high-resolution high-stability CCD spectrometers (UV, VIS and NIR).

Their laboratory and pharmacy specific refrigerators stored their stable experimental samples and the other various agents and compounds used in Project 4.20. They also helped preserve vaccines, reagents, serums, and multipurpose items that required different environments. The units were designed to exceed US efficiency guidelines. Each unit had three-pane thermally dynamic doors designed to minimize heat penetration and maintain clear visibility. The interiors contained non-conductive, epoxy-coated wire shelves with half-inch adjustable increments. Everything was built with state of the art construction materials.

There were semi-hermetic condensing units that allowed accurate product temperature measurement and control. Microprocessors electronically controlled temperature and defrost. Alarms could be set to monitor at the unit level or at a remote monitoring station.

Anything they didn't have was just a phone call away.

They were now about eleven weeks into their project. Julie had more or less transferred the role of mother to Pachita and the rest of the parenting tasks to Clark, but she kept her cell phone with her at all times just in case someone needed her. She asked her family not to disturb her at work, however, unless there was something really important that needed her immediate attention.

She was generally very careful about her lab behavior. She'd been a lab rat for years and knew how critical it was to keep detailed records, segregating samples in separate rooms, and keeping things clean and orderly. Accidents in labs can be deadly. She wore gloves. Everything was logged daily. Record-keeping was extremely accurate.

One evening, after weeks of extraordinarily long days, Julie was starting to feel fatigue setting in. She was tired and feeling a bit flighty. Her concentration was beginning to wane. She hadn't had much sleep over the past eight days, and much of it had been on her office couch. She hadn't been eating well, either. She had part of a package of cheese peanut butter crackers in her pocket.

She had been working on some of the spores from the Schumann Resonance Exposed Psilocybin-Schlorocia Pineal G-219-Serotonin-31 Hybrid, with the lab-name SREPSPG-19-S-31. She had a small vial of it next to her microscope and her phone was sitting on the lab table along with it. The vial of SREPSPG-19-S-31 had a glass stopper with a gasket to keep the contents air- and watertight. She had taken a small sample from the vial and was putting it on a slide when her phone went off. Julie heard the ring tone associated with their home phone number, Sly Stone's *It's a Family Affair*. It was unusual and unsettling.

Whenever that number came up on her phone, it was accompanied by a photograph of Clark, Philip, Peter, Heidi and herself, all sitting around a fire pit they had in their backyard. Her first thought was that she wished she were home with her family. The second thought was why the call and why at this hour. It was 6:30 in the evening. They all knew she was more or less in lock down.

She put the vial in her lab coat pocket without thinking and picked up the call. It was Peter. He was screaming.

"Dad's cut off his finger and has passed out on the floor! There is blood everywhere! Dad's not waking up! What should I do mom, what should I do?! I'm scared, Mom, there's blood splattered everywhere."

Julie said, "Calm down Peter, calm down. Did you call 911?"

"Yeah, Mom," Peter said, "Then I called you."

"Great job, Peter," Julie said. "Tell me what happened."

"Dad was making some guacamole, I think, and the knife slipped and cut his finger. It made a really big cut. Pachita is not here and Philip's not back from basketball."

"Peter," Julie said, "get a big wad of paper towels and try to wrap them around Dad's finger. I'll be there in a few minutes. Just try to be calm and stay close to Dad. He'll wake up in a minute. It's probably just shock. Dad will be fine."

"What's shock, Mom?" Peter asked.

"It means his body went to sleep really, really fast," Julie told him. "Dad will wake up in a couple of minutes. Just try to relax. When he wakes up get him a small glass of orange juice. I'll be right there, Peter. Just watch Dad and be in charge until I get there. I'm sure everything will be fine."

Julie ran to her office, grabbed her purse and keys, and ran for the door. She bent down to badge out.

Ned the security guard said, "Dr. Perthuis, you're still wearing your lab coat."

Julie, not stopping, said breathlessly over her shoulder, "Ned, there's been an accident. I have to hurry."

She tore out of the parking lot in her tan 540i, narrowly missing several of the concrete curbs. As she drove, she wrestled with fear for her husband's condition and guilt over not being there for him or her children. Not just tonight, when the situation was suddenly acute, but for three months, her absence had been chronic and near-complete. She hoped that Peter was exaggerating about Clark cutting *off* his finger. She cursed the circumstances that her son was facing now, the gore and the panic.

She was home in five minutes without a ticket. She'd been really flying.

The fire department was just arriving. Julie waved them to the kitchen door as she opened it. Clark was leaning up against the wall. He was conscious now, but there was blood everywhere. Peter had calmed down considerably, although he was pale.

Peter said, "Look, Mom, nice splatter, just like I told you. It's just like in CSI Miami."

"Very funny," Clark said.

Clark had put his finger back in place and wrapped it in a clean linen kitchen towel, but he knew this cut was going to require many stitches. Julie tossed her lab coat on the dining-room table and went to Clark. She gave him a kiss. Then she lifted his hand out of the bowl of bloody ice and peeled back the blood-soaked towel.

She gestured with her chin at the ice. "Good thinking." The chill would help stanch the blood loss and keep Clark's finger from deteriorating before it could be repaired.

"I'm a doctor," Clark smiled. "I learned that in med school 101."

"This is one nasty gash. Let's get you going before you lose any more blood," Julie commanded.

"Peter, you come with us so you are not here by yourself," Julie ordered.

"No," Peter said. "I should stay here with Heidi and wait for Philip. What'll he think if he walks in the house and sees all of this blood?"

Julie thought for a minute. "You're right. Go upstairs and watch the real CSI or a movie or something. I'll call you in a few minutes after we get to the hospital. Maybe put a frozen pizza in the oven or have some ice cream. I'll be back as soon as I can," Julie said.

Julie gave Peter a big hug, and so did Clark.

Clark said with a big smile, "Peter don't hug me too hard, I don't want to squirt any more blood around the room."

Julie gave Clark an admonishing glare.

But Peter said, "Yeah, sure, Dad. I've watched enough CSI to know that's not going to happen."

The EMTs stabilized the wound and off they went to the closest hospital. Clark knew everyone there, so they whisked him right in. Two hours and eighteen stitches later they were on their way back home.

When they arrived, the boys ran downstairs to see how their dad was doing. Everything is going to be fine said Clark. It was nothing a few stitches and some antibiotics couldn't fix.

Julie said, "Clark, you have to be as hungry as I am, how about a sandwich or something?"

"Sure," said Clark.

When she walked toward the kitchen, she saw her lab coat on the floor. During all the chaos, no one had fed Heidi. Heidi had fed herself. The partially eaten cheese peanut crackers were gone, and the vial had been gnawed open. Its contents were also gone. Presumably, Heidi had also eaten that, too. She was in the back yard, lying on one of the lounge chairs, looking at the sky.

Julie thought to herself, *Oh fuck!*

Chapter Seventeen

The next morning, everyone was fine. Clark's finger was in a bandage, the excitement of the accident had more or less worn off, and the kitchen was a mess. The cleaning people and Pachita would clean up the kitchen. Clark would try to go to work. Fortunately, it was his left hand. The boys went off to school.

Heidi was lethargic. She seemed alert, but wasn't running around as she usually did when her flock left the house. She seemed fine, though. Julie put some water in a bowl for Heidi, who quickly drank it all. As she refilled the bowl, Julie thought, *That dog will eat literally anything.*

Julie didn't have time to give Heidi much thought, however; she was thinking more about the long list of rules she had broken and the reports she would have to complete. There was a lot of bureaucratic paperwork ahead of her. She had to document how she had violated protocol in such a big way. The first thing she did was to make notes in her log that a vial of SREPSPG-19-S-31 had been lost. She noted the reasons, her inattention to HGMP Protocol Section 10, paragraph 3, point 4, and the precipitating event that caused the human error. Then, she called Paulo and said she needed ten minutes.

First, she updated Paulo on their progress and then she told him what had happened the night before.

Paulo smiled. "You mean to tell me that your dog actually ate your homework? That's actually pretty funny. Lucky you don't have a final grade riding on it. How's the pooch?"

Julie said, "as far as I can tell, our lunatic dog is fine. Heidi has demonstrated conclusively that she will eat anything. I am surprised she didn't eat the vial itself."

Paulo confirmed that Julie had logged the protocol violation. The chief compliance officer was informed. Paulo told Julie to be more careful in the future and since there was no apparent damage to forget about it. As far as Paulo was concerned, the case was closed. He did not see a need to bring Reynolds into this little incident. He did wonder, though, *What do dogs think about when they are tripping?*

Although Reynolds was not apprised of the security breach, unbeknownst to everyone at HGMP, others were aware of it. One of Wikileaks' most skilled hackers had been monitoring activity at HGMP for months now. John was particularly interested in Project 4.20. Although John respected much of what HGMP did, he was no fan of Bellihurton. On the contrary, he blamed them for many of the world's current problems.

John read the report, sat up in his bed, closed his laptop. and mused, *Chaos theory strikes again.* He had a powerful feeling in his gut that the law of unintended consequences was about to raise its head.

The work continued at HGMP at a feverish pace. Eighteen-hour days were the norm. Jimmy benefited greatly from Earp's research. Suzie, Jimmy, and Niconor were dedicated and fully committed to their ambitious deadline and the very big bonuses riding on getting it completed on time. They were thrilled to be tilling new soil. No one had done research like this. No one had ever been up in this neck of the woods. If evolution was slow, they had picked up the pace.

In the scant few months they'd been working, they had narrowed down the relevant pineal genes to 27 from 600. They had magnified the potency of the active ingredient in SREPSPG-19-S-31 by a full order of magnitude by pumping into its frequency-enhanced growing chamber an amped-up 7.83 Hz. The results were truly remarkable. The fungi were reproducing at extremely rapid rates, almost like cancer cells. They expanded their research to include a range of new hybrids. They were into a whole new world. In the world of lab-work, this was exciting. They knew they were on to something.

It had been about a month since Clark almost whacked off his finger. Reynolds was envisioning a world that where he and his people would finally be able to discreetly identify the infidels. He saw a Christian-based World Order forming before his eyes. His hopes and dreams, and those of his financiers, seemed to be falling in place. He was a proud and confident man, feeling that he was in reach of new tools that would change the world.

Chapter Eighteen

Heidi continued to be the normal English Setter the family had come to know and love. She slept at the bottom of the beds of Philip, Peter, or Clark. Julie had been in overdrive for almost three months now. The 4.20 project was arduous and, as predicted, Julie had not been home for reasons other than to sleep in her own bed once in a while or get changes of clothing. When she told Clark and the boys she'd be out of the picture for a few months, she hadn't been kidding. She was in full immersion mode.

Clark decided to take the boys on vacation to Jackson Hole, Wyoming. He planned to meet some old friends for a week of hiking, biking, and relaxing. He wanted Julie to fly in for a day but wasn't getting his hopes up. Maybe Paulo could arrange for one of his super-rich pals or clients to lend her a G-4 for the trip.

Since biking was part of the planned activities, Clark decided to make it a road trip. They'd hop in the big blue Suburban and cruise across the Great Plains. I-80 was a pretty straight shot. They would stop in Salt Lake City and other points of interest, wiggling their way to Jackson Hole. Philip and Peter were super-excited. They just wished that their mom could come too.

Clark's old friend was a pal from med school. He and his wife had two boys about the same ages as Philip and Peter. The Percivals were from Pittsburgh, Pennsylvania. The two families had vacationed once before on the island of St. John. They lived in platform tents that overlooked a beautiful bay in the Caribbean. Everyone got along just fine. This time there would be no Julie, but two dogs. It should be fun, Clark thought.

The Percivals decided to do the same and also make it a road trip. I-80 worked well for them too. They would stop in Chicago and then drive through America's great breadbasket, Iowa and Nebraska. If you added up all the food products that came from Iowa, Nebraska, and California, it made up something like sixty-five percent of the US supply. Thousands of tons of food, fertilizer, seeds, and livestock were also shipped around the globe. It was a very important part of the world's food supply.

It was also a long, straight boring drive, but perfect for catching up on old movies, an audiobook or two, and lots of music. In addition to their two boys, the Percivals were bringing along their dog Tuffy, a Dalmatian. Heidi and Tuffy would have a good time running around the house that Clark had rented.

They each were off with dogs in tow, heading to the same place from opposite ends of the map. They would drive well over a thousand miles to reach their destination, and then the same for the return legs. Each family had its schedule, planned places to camp or stay in a motel or hotel and they would rendezvous in Jackson Hole in a week.

Chapter Nineteen

Unless you were a dog walker or dog-poop picker-upper, the area surrounding Palo Alto seemed largely unchanged over the past eight weeks. But if you happened to fall into either of these two categories and if you were moderately observant, there was something very unusual going on. There were little mushrooms sprouting out of dogshit, and it wasn't just Heidi's shit. These small mushrooms were popping up all over the place, either where there was or had been dog poop. Rob the dog walker knew because Dr. Perthuis was one of his clients. Rob was Heidi's walker five days a week, seven now that Julie was on a special project and not home for the husband and wife walks that Clark and Julie enjoyed on the weekends. Rob had first spotted the little mushrooms in the Perthuis' back yard, but didn't give them a second thought. Lots of things sprouted up in the glorious California climate.

Rob had a reasonably fixed routine. He would enter the Perthuis's home with his key, get Heidi's leash from the kitchen drawer, and off they'd go for fifteen minutes or so. When Rob and Heidi returned, Heidi would perform her ritual sprint around the kitchen and then gallop into the back yard. Rob would bring her back into the house, give her a biscuit, write a note and then move on to his next client. Rob did this for about a dozen families each day. It was the ultimate no-preparation-needed-for-tomorrow job. Just show up more or less on time and interact with a bunch of dogs. You could be half-asleep, stoned, hungover, pissed off, or whatever. All you had to do was get there, walk the dogs, and jot a mindless note to the dogs' owners. Typically, Rob would write something like, "Heidi had a nice walk and was happy. Lots of wags. She went #1 and #2. Rob."

Rob was an aspiring actor/musician who had a bachelor's degree in botany. His real goal in life was to get his money for nothing and his chicks for free. He wanted to be a professional musician, not Clapton, not P Diddy, not Sting, but successful enough to support himself and a family in a comfortable lifestyle. He didn't aspire to have Oprah money, just enough money for a healthy and relaxed life without stressful financial worries. He certainly didn't want fame. In his heart of hearts, he really wanted to be rich and obscure, but he recognized the long odds. He just didn't want to have to worry about money. So to sidestep the problem, at least for the moment, he elected to be poor. As of the moment, his life and lifestyle were relaxed. He was healthy, had lots of free time, and some of his best friends were dogs.

Although Rob had an affinity for botany, he did not want to spend the required five plus additional years in school getting his Masters and PhD. He liked his time. Each morning Rob would get up around nine, make a cup of espresso, and do a bong hit or two. Then he'd grab his 1964 Gibson Hummingbird and play guitar until his buzz wore off. After that, he'd grab one of the many partially read books he had strewn all over his cluttered apartment. He was an inveterate reader, but rarely finished any book he picked up. He read books on finance, Western European history, lots of philosophy, but most writers just didn't capture his full enthusiasm or attention for that matter. But he read a lot. He did finish Keith Richard's book *Life* and Ray Kurzweil's *The Age of Spiritual Machines*, but these were exceptions. He had a curious but unfocused mind. Through his dog-walking gig, he made almost enough money to pay his rent. He also sold a little weed on the side to stay out of debt, but was almost always a day late and a dollar short.

As often as he could motivate himself to do it, Rob would go to the open mic sessions at local coffee shops and bars. He'd sign up on the slotting sheet and then go smoke a joint. When his name was called, he'd take his guitar out of its case and walk to the stage, take a seat on the chair set up for performers, and play two or three songs. Some were original compositions and others were covers. He did a great rendition of Bob Dylan's "It Takes a Lot to Laugh and a Train to Cry." And when he played Doc Watson's "Walk On Boy," he always got great applause and lots of cheers. It didn't hurt that he looked a little like Johnny Depp or Paul Dano. He had that lanky, indie-pop-singer-songwriter image. Usually wore a black shirt and jeans. It was a good look. Women loved him.

Beyond his musical interests, Rob was also one highly observant fellow. Due in part to his interest in botany, he usually kept his eyes directed toward the ground when he walked. He divided the human race into two groups, those who looked at the ground when they walked and those who looked elsewhere. Rob was a devout ground-watcher. He loved plants, fungi, sidewalk graffiti, and grasses. He loved the dirt and the trash. He loved cracks in the sidewalks. He paid attention to dogshit when he had to pick it up with plastic bags and then tossed it into the closest garbage can.

Rob began to notice fungi on dogshit that had not been picked up. It looked the same as the little mushrooms he had seen in Julie's back yard. Rob had walked dogs for two years and his family had dogs when he was young. He could not recall seeing anything happen to dogshit except that it eventually dried up, if left untouched long enough. Now, he saw something new. There were little mushrooms popping up out of day-old poop. At first, this didn't strike Rob as too odd. Rob knew enough about biology and botany to know that life forms have a way of finding a medium to allow for their own survival. The more he thought about it, however, the more it seemed strange to him. Rob knew mushrooms grew on cow dung, but not dogshit. This was new.

He knew that fungi have been part of the earth's ecosystem for 1.3 billion years, give or take. So, at first Rob thought, some new mushroom, BFD. He remembered studying one particular mushroom, Armillaria ostoyae, which is actually the largest living organism on earth. This single specimen resides in the state of Oregon, covering an area of 2,384 acres.

Rob always thought the fungus was a weird life form. Some were also very closely related to bacteria and could reproduce and spread with astonishing speed. Some behaved like viruses. Others formed very powerful symbiotic relationships with other plants, insects, and animals. There were probably 600,000 varieties of fungi on earth. Now there are 600,001 or whatever, he thought.

But why a new one now and why here?

Chapter Twenty

Rob made a mental note of the new dogshit mushroom variety. As he walked dogs for people who were either too busy or too lazy to do the job themselves, he continued to see the odd little mushrooms. But what was more interesting to him was that he now saw them on a daily basis. Very unusual. He decided to collect a few samples and find out what kind of mushroom it was.

He went back to his apartment and pulled out his old copy of *A Pocket Guide to North American Mushrooms*. The book's page ends were marked by silhouettes of mushroom shapes. The pages were ordered in a shape-based sequence. It was easy for Rob to thumb through the pages, going from tall and skinny mushrooms to the shorter and fatter ones until he found some that were similar in shape to the ones he'd collected. To his astonishment, they resembled the psilocybin mushroom. His mushrooms weren't exactly the same as the psilocybin mushrooms, but they more closely resembled them than any of the others. *Now this is really fucking weird*, he thought. *I need some help.*

He still had some friends from college, a professor and a former girlfriend who was now a doctoral student in mycology. He decided to take the samples to his crazy ex-girlfriend, just for the fun of it. He also decided to not tell them where they came from. Instead, he'd say that someone had sold him these 'shrooms and he wanted to make sure they weren't poisonous before he ate them. He figured Sally would be happy to run a few tests and find out what they were. He also expected her to say something like, "Rob, I guess you're getting old and conservative or scared or something. What happened to the guy I used to know who would pop anything in his mouth just in case it got him high?"

Rob thought about Sally and a wave of great memories rushed through his head. Sally was a very interesting thrill-seeker type and a great-looking, sexy woman, a brunette with a great athletic figure. She and Rob met during the summer when they were each taking their break from the University of Michigan. They met in the unlikeliest of places, Three Oaks, Michigan. Three Oaks is a tiny farm town surrounded by corn and soybeans, but it is a cute and artsy little place, kind of like Mayberry but with art galleries and good food. The entire town is two blocks long. Three Oaks also has a small theater called the Acorn. The Acorn Theater has open mic sessions, and Rob would occasionally take the stage and try out some of his songs. The venue was extremely cool, with theater seating, a nice elevated stage, a good sound system, and good sound technicians. It was the ideal spot to try to develop music and stage craft. Rob called it "the greatest place in the world to fuck up." He played some good music, and Sally took a liking to Rob.

After his set one night, she introduced herself. "Hi there, Rob. My name's Sally. I really liked your music," she said. "That finger picking is really cool. Just great."

"Thanks a lot," he said. "Can I get you a beer or a drink?"

"A glass of water, hold the ice," Sally said with an inviting smile.

"Sure. I'll be right back."

One thing led to another, and they went down the street to the local diner for a burger. The burgers and fries were pretty good, smothered in grilled onions, but they really hit it off with each other. They talked about music. Sally's favorite current player was Jack Johnson. Rob's was John Mayer. They were each huge fans of Johnny Mercer whom they considered to be the greatest contemporary songwriter. They talked a little politics, tossed around a few funny one-liners, and at some point Rob turned the conversation to alcohol.

"So Sally, how come you don't drink? You have to be the only college kid in the world who doesn't," Rob said almost aggressively.

"I like acid," Sally said. "And I really enjoy banging while tripping," she added calmly but with an inviting smile. "Particularly the first time," she said.

Rob was speechless and almost spit out his beer. Sally's candor and sexual aggression were so unexpected that he didn't quite know how to respond. Rob had never taken acid, but had smoked plenty of good weed and drank a bit.

And after a line like that, Sally went off on a short rant, "I've drunk enough alcohol to have concluded it the most dangerous and destructive drug on the planet. It's the ultimate gateway drug. Five percent of deaths in our country are directly related to drinking. Drinking costs the economy, just the US economy, fourteen billion dollars each year in decreased productivity and accidents. The whole industry just pisses me off. Who smokes a joint or takes acid and then decides to rob a gas station? Nobody. It's the booze."

Sally stayed on her soapbox for five minutes, or so it seemed. Rob was afraid to look at his watch, but listened anxiously and looked awkwardly at his half-empty glass of beer.

Sally said, "I have very little tolerance for over-served drunks. I think it's escapism for amateurs and I don't enjoy being around them. And it's too bad for me, because it gets harder and harder to do each year. More and more people just drink and drink and drink. It's too much. It's just a waste."

Then, without hesitation, Sally said, "So, are you up for it? Want to join me?"

And with that stunning invitation, she opened her purse, pulled out two tiny tablets and placed them on a napkin.

"Really good stuff, nice and clean. I know the chemist. About six hours," she said.

"Sure," Rob said without delay.

And they each popped the little orange pills in their mouths.

Rob was elated that he had taken Sally up on her offer and it was the best sex he'd ever had and the best consciousness he's ever experienced. The sex, actually, was secondary to his newfound state of mind. The door had been opened. Rob was now an acid-head. He went on to try a wide range of hallucinogens with Sally. It was the very best summer of his life. Rob remained a drinker, however, and over time, Sally lost her patience with him. Consequently, her interest in a serious relationship with him faded. They parted good friends in the end. They were each sad about it. In Sally's view Rob's inability to dump John Barleycorn was proof positive that her view was correct. For Rob, Sally was simply too inflexible. They did stay in touch, but they also each moved on.

Now, years later, sitting in his cluttered apartment, Rob grabbed his cell phone from the coffee table and dialed Sally's number from his contacts list.

"Sally, this is Rob," he said. "How are you doing? How's the dissertation coming along?"

There was a pause that was slightly too long.

"Rob, how are you? Long time no talk. Good to hear your voice. I'm just fine. Thanks for asking. And the dissertation.... well it's progressing. I told my dad I'd have it done this year and he replied, 'that's what you said last year.' But, I think I might actually get it wrapped up," she said. "What's up? What brings you out of the blue?"

"Well," Rob said, "I've got a mushroom sample and I'm wondering if you'd take a look at it, tell me what it is and specifically, if it's safe. You never know. It's not like buying scotch."

"Nice one, Rob," Sally said. "Sure, I'd be happy to take a look. Where and when?"

"How about RawDaddy's? I'll treat you to a mushroom polenta cone," Rob quipped.

"Still quick on your feet, or did you have that one already teed up?"

"Right off the top," Rob replied. "When?"

"I'm good for the next few hours, just grading some tests for Earp," she said.

"How's that crazy character doing?" Rob asked.

"He's as crazy and brilliant and acerbic as ever. I am blessed and cursed to be part of his world," Sally replied.

"Glad to hear it. How about in an hour?" Rob asked.

"See you then," Sally said.

When she walked through the restaurant's door, she looked as appealing as ever. She was wearing a reasonably tight pair of jeans, some perfectly worn black Lucchese cowboy boots, a blue buttoned down cotton shirt, no bra, and turquoise earrings with matching cufflinks. *She was hot,* Rob thought regretfully.

"Great to see you, Sally." Rob stood up and gave her a social kiss on the cheek, adding in his best Billy Crystal imitation, "You look marvelous."

Sally sat down across from him in the booth and grabbed both his hands. "You, too," she said.

"You look kind of uptown for a doctoral student, or did you have this change of clothes hanging in your office closet in case I called?" Rob asked.

"Don't flatter yourself," Sally replied. "We had the provost visiting the department this morning, so I dolled it up a bit. Never hurts, you know."

"No doubt," Rob said without averting his gaze.

Sally's eyes were electric green. Vibrant and exhilarating. They delivered the clear message that there was a very sharp mind behind them. "You look pretty good yourself. The dogs must be taking good care of you," Sally said with a smile.

"Oh, they do. They get me off the couch and they've given me the best conversations on accrual accounting I've ever had," he said.

They chatted for about a half an hour as they had strawberry cheesecake cones and some coffee.

Then Sally changed the subject. "So, dude, where'd you get the magic?" Her tone combined interest and sarcasm.

"You know, some guy after a gig. I just want to check them out. I've never seen any that look like these. There are about twelve grams. I'm anxious to try them in the truest senses of the word," Rob said.

"Okay, lay 'em on me, bro," she joked.

Rob handed Sally a Starbucks coffee bag containing his sample of dogshit 'shrooms.

"How professional and discreet," Sally said. "I'll get back to you after I've run some tests."

125

"Thanks, Sally," Rob said. "Really good to see you."

"You too, Rob."

Sally took the sample 'shrooms back to her office and closed the door. She got a white glass dish and a few wide-mouth glass containers with airtight lids from her wall cabinet. She dumped the contents of the small plastic bag into the dish and turned on the magnifying glass with its built-in halogen light source. She maneuvered the magnifying glass over the plate and took a studious look, turning the sample various ways with her tweezers. *Rob was right,* she immediately thought. *These are new to me, anyway. I've never seen anything quite like this. Curious.*

She started by running them through a standard battery of tests to isolate their chemical makeup and help dictate what, if any, additional analysis would be needed. The analytical process was pretty much like the stuff you see on TV crime shows. She took a sample, ground it into a powder, and added an inert liquid solution to create slurry. She put the slurry in a centrifuge to separate the elements based on their specific weights, and then matched those components to chemical profiles in a database designed specifically for this purpose. Oxygen, if found, would match the oxygen profile in the database. Potassium, if present, matched potassium, and so on. Sally figured these mushrooms would be similar in composition to psilocybin, the 'shrooms that she and Rob had enjoyed when they were together during their summer of love.

When the data came back, there were specific compound spikes so high on the graph that they fouled up the Y-axis. The sample contained the active ingredient found in psilocybin, 4-hydroxyl-dimethyltryptamine, but in a concentration a hundred times greater than found in the psilocybin mushroom. If that finding were not enough to grab Sally's attention, NDM-1 was also found in the sample. NDM-1 is commonly found in E. coli, which is a common source of community-acquired infections, and K. pneumonia. Congregate environments such as schools, hospitals, prisons, gymnasiums, etc. were the ideal setting for rapid dispersal of anything attached to them. NDM-1 is also impervious to all antibiotics except tigecycline and colistin. In some cases, even these drug regimens could not inhibit the progress of an infection. Significantly, the NDM-1 gene was found on DNA structures called plasmids. These plasmids can be easily replicated and passed along to other organisms or bacteria, giving NDM-1 the frightening potential to spread and, equally significant, diversify.

As far as Sally could tell, NDM-1 had attached itself to the spore's genes. An unknown virus had also done the same. This implied that the spore could reproduce and spread with relative ease three-dimensionally using three distinct mechanisms, normal biological-based reproduction, viral reproduction and distribution, and bacterial reproduction and distribution. This appeared to be one complex and dangerous substance. She spent hours researching various compounds and combing the web for anything that might be helpful. Eventually, she looked at her watch and was alarmed to see it was almost two in the morning. She closed her eyes, burning from prolonged overuse.

Sally had never seen anything quite like this before and decided to send her professor and dissertation advisor, Dr. Earp, a note with the data she'd developed so far and then call it an evening.

By dawn, Earp was equally intrigued. As far as they could determine, this was a new life form. It was not only new, it was biologically strong, genetically expressive, and had staggering potential for exponential growth. As far as Sally and Dr. Earp knew, there were no known fungicides to impede its growth or slow dispersion. This was new stuff.

Sally called Rob. "Rob, where did you say you got these?"

"Like I told you, some dude, I don't know him real well, came up to me after a gig and offered me a sample. I said thanks and told him I check them out. Why?"

"Rob, we've never seen anything like these. If you are going to eat them, do so with care and have some Xanax handy, just in case. I'd also recommend not eating more than one, or maybe eat just a small part of one. They appear to be exceptionally powerful. They also appear to be able to grow and reproduce extremely easily. Be careful. These things look wild. We've never seen anything even remotely like this."

"Absolutely, Sally. Want to join me?"

Sally paused and said with a note of humor, "I'll wait for your review. Still drinking?"

Rob said, "Yeah, but not as much."

"Too bad," Sally said.

Rob went home and thought about how nice it was to see Sally again. She was smart, witty, and sexy. It was too bad he had screwed up things and too bad she couldn't have been a little more flexible or understanding of his needs.

Rob then thought, *Maybe there is a new source of income for me. If these things are half as potent as Sally suspects, this could be a really nice find. I'd be a hero and I wouldn't have to deal with the purchasing side of a drug deal.* That always made him nervous. From a financial angle, this was just free money. All he had to do was harvest. First, though, he needed to actually see what this stuff was like. The next day was Rob's day off. He was about to learn a new meaning of "off."

Rob took a walk along his dog walker route until he spotted one of the dogshit 'shrooms. He pinched it a little bit above the turd, took it home, rinsed it gently under running water, dried it with a paper towel, cut it in half and popped a half into his mouth. Before the little piece of the mushroom had hit the back of his soft palette, he was feeling some kind of effect. His heart rate was increasing and the light seemed brighter. He guessed that his pupils were dilating. Within three minutes, he was having intense, full-blown hallucinations as beautiful and overwhelming as anything he had experienced or read about.

He went outside, collapsed on a lounge chair, and watched the insects and the clouds. He heard the birds singing and talking to each other. He looked at the dog in the neighbor's yard; he was convinced they were bonding. He had a vision of universal harmony and world peace. He had a vision of all of mankind experiencing the same feeling at the same time and wondered what would happen to the world if there were that kind of universal human experience, a sort of species-wide hallucination. What kind of energy would that create? Similar things happened at Grateful Dead concerts, but with only ten thousand people all tripping at the same time. What would happen if three billion people simultaneously tripped on this stuff?

This was a transcendental experience in the truest sense of the word. He believed he had seen his reason for living. He believed he now knew the meaning of life. Then, like a light switch being turned off, it was over. He felt as if he's been travelling for an eternity across time and space. He checked his watch and only forty minutes had passed. Even though it was just ten in the morning, Rob had a beer. As far as he knew, there was one person alive who really knew what he had discovered, and it was him. It was a remarkable and energizing feeling. Now what?

With ever an eye for the fast buck with little work involved, Rob went 'shroom picking. He started at the dog park. Within an hour, he had a freezer bag full of the tiny dogshit 'shrooms. He guessed it weighed about a pound and that he had five hundred or so of them. Based on his experience they had to be worth at least twenty bucks each. He had ten grand worth of 'shrooms if they were sold at retail. Selling that much retail was way more work and way more risk than he had in mind, so he called his favorite pot supplier, Skippy, and said he wanted to connect later in the day.

Skippy said, "Any time man, I'm just hangin', dude. Come on over and party."

Rob took about a tenth of the bag over to Skippy's house.

Skippy said, "What's happening, man? Want some green? I've got this like killer, super-killer weed, better than any of the dispensary shit. Really killer."

Rob said, "Yeah, maybe, and I've got some unbelievable 'shrooms."

"Whoa, cool dude. They're getting popular again. So is acid, but they're not so easy to get," Skippy said.

Rob said, "Well, this guy I know has a line on these 'shrooms and isn't quite sure what they are worth. I'm not sure either, because they are like a hundred times more powerful than anything I've have ever taken. Yesterday I tripped like I was from another fucking galaxy. Here, try one. Actually, let's split it." Rob broke a small one in half.

Skippy said, "Get the fuck out of here with that little thing. I'll take a whole one."

"Suit yourself, but fasten your seatbelt, because you're going to be off in about three minutes."

"Yeah, sure," Skippy said, "Let me have one."

Within three minutes, they were both higher than an Apollo astronaut and higher than either of them had ever been. Rob followed Skippy's lead and took a whole cap. They were really, really sailing. When they looked at each other, they thought they could hear each other thinking. When they closed their eyes, they thought they could still see each other. They were rolling around on the floor laughing their asses off. They got into a fly-catching contest, to see who could catch more flies with his hands. Catching flies is usually tricky and difficult. They were catching them like they were worms. Whatever this shit was, it was remarkably strong and totally different from anything either of them had ever experienced. After an hour, presto-chango, they were back to normal.

Laughing, Skippy said, "Whoa, dude! Like, what the fuck was that?! That was, like, the best fucking trip I've ever been on. I mean, like, dude, like that was, like, fucking amazing. I'll never be the same again. Like, I was in a place that I can't even, like, describe. It was like I was in your head and you were in mine. We were on a like, a rollercoaster or something, and now I'm, like, back to, like, complete normal, no hangover or anything. Wherever your friend found these things, I hope he can find more of them. I'd say they are worth about twenty-five bucks apiece on the street, and if you've got any weight, I'll give you ten bucks each for them."

Rob said, "How about twelve, so I can make a little."

"Sure, dude, this shit is fucking awesome. I'll take whatever you have in that bag and whatever you can find. I can move as much of this as you can deliver."

They counted out the remaining 'shrooms, on the kitchen table. The table was cluttered with weed and paraphernalia: papers, matches, a scale, a bong, a couple of pipes, plastic bags, empty orange pills bottles, the usual stuff. Their count in Rob's bag was fifty 'shrooms. Skippy gave Rob six hundred bucks and told him to come back as soon as you can with more—these would be gone in a few hours.

Rob came back the next day with the rest of his bag and Skippy gave Rob another $5400. Rob couldn't believe what he'd stumbled into. Rob now had six grand and the day before he'd had zero. He knew one thing for sure; he had to play it cool, really cool.

Chapter Twenty-One

R ob thought through his situation. First, there was some significant and very quick money to be made. Second, it was just a matter of time until someone else figured out that these 'shrooms were free and for the taking. Third, once that was figured out two things would happen—his money making opportunities would dry up, and there would be some kind of law enforcement, military, hazmat, political response. That was certain. It would be a big response, no question, but the timing, message, and impact were unpredictable.

Rob decided he needed to make hay while the sun was shining and hope for the best. Rob decided he would cap his sales to Skippy at 2500 units a week. Rob also had a friend in Nashville where he could do the same. Rob called his buddy and gave him the scoop and also told him that if he didn't like the product to just send them back FedEx. After his buddy received the first batch, he called Rob.

"Dude," he said "This is the greatest, most far-out shit I have ever, ever had. Absolutely mind-blowing. I'll take as much as you can get."

Rob said, "I thought you'd like them. I'll send you as much as I can, but just keep it cool, really cool. Don't buy anything, got it?"

"Yep. Got it," he said with the tone of a subordinate who'd just been given a very direct order.

Rob quickly developed a procedure to manage his packaging and shipping requirements. He used Mason jars. After carefully filling each Mason jar with his product, he tightly closed the lid, washed the closed jar with soap and very hot water. Then he dried them and wrapped each lid with duct tape. Rob then wrapped each jar with lots of bubble wrap and packed the jars in a box, taped it closed, addressed it, and put the ready-to-ship box in a large shopping bag with easy to carry handles. When he was all done, he removed his rubber gloves and walked over to the local FedEx office. Rob sent a box of 'shrooms to Nashville once a week via FedEx.

Within a few weeks, Rob was taking in about a hundred grand a month in cash. He had never seen so much money in his life. It was the easiest gig he had ever had. He picked the 'shrooms while he walked his dogs. He put them in plastic bags—the Ziploc ones used for sandwiches—repackaged them, and handed them off to just two people. Those two people gave him large sums of cash, in twenty-dollar bills. Rob was very paranoid and very smart about how he handled his new windfall of cash. He didn't change one thing about his lifestyle. He looked and acted like the same down-on-his-luck-almost-starving-actor/musician he'd been for years. Rob didn't buy any guitars or amps or new clothing. He was the same guy in the eyes of anyone else. He even paid some of his bills late and partially paid his landlord specifically to keep everything real. This went on for about two months. Rob then had accumulated about a half a million dollars in cash. He buried most of it in his parents' back yard.

His parents had a nice home in the area and his mother had a large garden that needed lots of tending and regular work. Rob had been a helpful son for years, giving his mom a hand in the yard whenever he could. Consequently, Rob's digging around in the garden was a common sight. There were lots of grasses, rhododendron, lilies, dozens of deciduous trees, and also firs. There was always work to be done, trimming, weeding, raking, picking up dead branches, and so on. He had excellent cover for digging a few holes and dropping in boxes full of money.

He used small Rubbermaid containers about 14x8x14 inches. They had been made for storing files and had a snap on green lid. They were reasonably airtight, but Rob put the money in freezer bags first and then used duct tape to fully seal the top. He was confident the money would be safe from deterioration for decades. To make sure he wouldn't forget what he'd done, he first mapped out the location of the holes using a grid. He had ten holes sketched out. Every time he had a new container of money, he went over to help his mom. When Mom went to the store or took a walk, he quickly dug his hole, dropped in the box, planted a flower or something on top of it, and it was gone. He kept a little notebook with some cryptic notations on which holes had been used, guitar-chord shapes reflecting the grids he had drawn. No one else could possibly figure it out.

The research at HGMP was fruitful. Their hybrid building had gone far beyond SREPSPG-19-S-31—the spores that Heidi had eaten and unwittingly spread across America's heartland. Julie and her team were now into version 4.0 of this specific strain. It was actually producing clairvoyant-like perceptions with high measures of accuracy.

Their tests were interesting and done in bi-directional settings. In one experimental design, the government's "perceiver" would ingest the agent. Then in another room, there would be twenty subjects. All the subjects were dressed the same and wore the same Halloween masks. They all wore white, long sleeve, extra large T-shirts, white shoes, white socks, and blue jeans. They were roughly the same somatotypes, and they wore long gloves and tinted glasses. It was not possible to identify the age, race or sex of the subjects. Subjects wore a random four-digit number that hung from their necks. This number had been printed on a cardboard plate, about the size of a car's license plate. Each subject sat in the same type of chair and his or her feet were to remain on the floor. From a viewer's perspective, they all looked more or less identical. They were told not to move and only to read once given the instruction to do so.

The "perceiver" sat on the viewer side of a one-way mirror. The subjects were each given folders with a page of reading material inside. Eighteen of the subjects had one story, the control group, and two of the subjects had a different story. This was the experimental group. The perceiver's job was to identify the two individuals with the experimental story. After the subjects had opened their envelopes, placed the sheet of paper on their desk surface, and put their hands on the desk top, the perceiver was able to view the room and look at each subject. With about eighty percent accuracy, the perceivers could ID the subjects with the experimental text. So far, they had used twenty different perceivers. The results were promising.

The other test methodology reversed the use of the psychoactive agent. That is, the perceiver was not dosed, but the subjects were. All of the other conditions were the same. So were the results. The perceivers were correct about eighty percent of the time. Promising results, but the performance was not reliable enough for field use, surviving legal challenges, widespread deployment, etc. They needed full reliability, one hundred percent accuracy.

Julie wondered what would happen if both the readers and the perceivers were each dosed with the compounds they were creating. This of course, might produce results exactly opposite the goals Reynolds had in mind. But if the compounds performed reliably and allowed for valid extra-sensory communication, HGMP would change the world.

Chapter Twenty-Two

Rob woke up and showered while his coffee was brewing. He had an odd fixation of using little bits of time as efficiently as possible. It was as if he were a short-order cook. He was kind of weird like that. Although he had plenty of time on his hands, he thought about ways to save time by doing two or three things at once. He'd put bread in the toaster, start the coffee and cook soft-boiled eggs, and take a shower all in the same four minutes. He just got cheap thrills out of stupid little timesavers. After he got his coffee, toast, and eggs, he sat down at his computer and went to his Yahoo homepage.

He looked at the big headlines and said, "Fuck."

There it was. Rob always knew it was just a matter of time until his little cash cow gig would come to a screeching halt, but there it was for one and all to see. The headline with photo read: "HIGHLY TOXIC AND DANGEROUS MUSHROOM FOUND IN CLEVELAND."

There was a picture of the little dogshit 'shroom. He clicked into the story. The Associated Press, in cooperation with the *Cleveland Plain Dealer*, had contributed the article.

AP, Cleveland, Ohio. An unusual, new, and highly dangerous and toxic mushroom has been discovered in Boardman, Ohio. The small mushroom, measuring about a half an inch in diameter and growing an inch to an inch and a half tall has been found throughout this working class suburb of Cleveland. Residents have been encouraged to take extra care to pick up dog droppings, as it appears this mushroom grows on or around dog feces. Although there have been no reported deaths, the Cleveland Memorial Clinic did report that a patient had been admitted after reporting intestinal distress and extreme psychological and emotional disorientation. The patient, whose name was not released, was discharged from the hospital late yesterday. Dr. Morris Adelman, Director of Virology and Bacterial Analysis with the Centers for Disease Control (CDC), said, "This organism is a new species of mushroom. Its toxicity levels are extremely high and fast-acting. We consider it to be extremely dangerous and encourage people to not touch these mushrooms with their bare hands and to call our hotline if they see it. Call: 1.800.CDC.HELP.

Rob had several thoughts: First, his little money machine was over. It would just be a matter of weeks now before everybody figured out how to get his 'shrooms for free. By Rob's rough reckoning though, based on his unit sales, about 40,000 people had tripped on his little 'shrooms. They were all the rage at raves and rock concerts in California and areas around Nashville. The Phish-heads were all over them. There was even a small, but funny "Trip and Tweet" communication circle. Because the 'shrooms' introduction to the market was so fast, and the use still relatively small and largely localized, they hadn't picked up much attention from the mainstream media. There had also been very few arrests, so the story was still unknown outside a small group. Rob really got a kick out of the whole thing because he was the only person who really knew the entire story. At least, he thought he knew the entire story.

Second, now that the CDC was involved, it wouldn't be long before the entire federal government would be involved. Third, and the most interesting thing for Rob, was that the 'shrooms were now in Cleveland. Rob expected the 'shrooms would be popular in and around Nashville where his friend had sold them, but Cleveland? *How the fuck did that happen?* Rob wondered. *Maybe Sally would have some idea*, he thought.

His cell phone vibrated. It was Sally's name on the screen.

"Sally, that's really weird—literally, I mean literally, I was just thinking about you. You didn't happen to see the story about Cleveland, did you?" Rob asked.

"Sure I did, Rob. I've also seen the "Trip and Tweet" activity. This seems oddly coincidental in light of the research I did for you and the results we found," Sally said, her tone an odd mix of confusion, irritation, and admiration. A long pause. "Anything you want to share?"

"Well I can't figure out how they got to Cleveland," Rob said, cutting to the chase with a tone of sincere curiosity. "The Twitter threads I can explain. I helped get it going. I mean, I might as well just tell you. I found that sample I gave to you right around here, right around my apartment. After you gave me the green light, I tried them. They were just fucking awesome. They're all over the place around here growing on dogshit. I started harvesting them. I have a couple friends in the distribution business and they took care of the rest. They've become very, very popular. But growing in Cleveland—that's just a weird coincidence I guess."

"Jesus," Sally said, deflated, as she was reflecting on her potential role in this now highly public episode. "And as for a coincidence with Cleveland, I kind of doubt it, Rob. I didn't share all of my findings with you. I didn't think you cared about the exact nature and characteristics of the sample beyond its psychotropic properties and if was safe, so that's all I told you. I figured you just wanted to get off. We also discovered that the sample had reproductive properties resembling viruses, and bacteria, as well as those usually associated with fungi. This means—"

Rob interrupted, "This means they can reproduce at least three ways and can't easily be killed?" he added with a sense of alarm and glee.

"Exactly," Sally said with a tone of excitement and fear.

"Sally, do you have any idea how they could have gotten to Cleveland?" Rob asked.

"They could have started there, for all I know," Sally said.

"Wow. Fuck. This could be—" and Rob started to laugh hysterically, "really wild."

Sally said, "I'll call you later. Earp's calling and I'm guessing I know why.

"Hello, Dr. Earp," said Sally.

"Okay. What's the rest of the story, Sally?" Earp demanded. "I read the news, too, and the Cleveland story sounds just a tad related to the work we did a while back for your old flame. You might as well spill the beans, because I've got a real strong feeling the fertilizer is ready to hit and I want to make goddamn sure I'm on the right side of the fan."

"Professor, I was just on the phone with that old flame," Sally said. "He told me more than I knew, but not enough to explain Cleveland. Get a load of this. That sample? He collected it right around here. He picked those samples off of dogshit. Off of fucking dogshit! Can you believe it? Then he started selling them. That explains the new tripping activity I've been reading about on Facebook. But the Cleveland discovery doesn't square with anything that I know."

"Okay," said Earp. He hung up and immediately dialed Julie Perthuis.

"Dr. Earp, good morning," she said. "What a nice surprise. Thanks again for that quick summary you sent a while back. It was very helpful."

"I'm glad to hear it," Earp said curtly. "Care to share what you've been up to? I might be able to help. I've been racing through the halls of psychotropia for longer than you've been alive and might be able to shed some light on whatever it is you are trying to do. I have a hunch you might find yourself under the microscope."

"The NIH research was terrific," Julie replied, not very convincingly. "It does appear some psychotropics might, in fact, cure severe alcoholism."

"Great. Glad to hear it. Maybe there's hope for me yet," he said sarcastically. "What do you know about Cleveland?"

"If you're referring to the CDC situation, I know what I've read and seen on the news," she said. "What do you think?"

"I think you might have an inkling of an idea about those strange mushrooms. The things are growing on dogshit. Fancy that," he said.

"I don't know anything, Wyatt," she said. "Really."

"Okay, beautiful. If you decide to come clean or need some help, you know where to reach me. Try not to catch any shrapnel." Earp said and hung up.

Julie got up from her chair and began pacing around her office. She looked at the sphere, but for just for a few seconds, and then resumed her uncharacteristically nervous pacing. She thought about her accident a few months ago. And she thought about Heidi eating her sample. Could these three things be related? Julie had been up working for about ten hours and was fatigued. She decided to take a quick nap. She had taught herself years ago how to go to sleep on command and to set an internal alarm to wake herself after so many minutes or so many hours of sleep. She would look at her watch, decide how long she wanted to sleep, add the sleep period to the current time, and then tell herself to wake up at a specific time, say ten fifteen, after having slept for whatever period she had decided upon. With frighteningly accurate and reliable results, she'd wake up exactly at that time, usually as the second hand swept past twelve. It was an amazing little trick. It actually creeped her out a bit because it was so accurate. She'd done it many times over the past two decades.

She set her phone to forward and turned off her cell ringer. She grabbed a lightweight throw that she kept in her office, put on her eye pillows to block out the light and set her mind for twenty minutes. Then she stretched out on her couch and was asleep in ninety seconds.

Ten minutes into her nap she woke with a start. *The dog food! That's what did it! How could I have missed it?* The dog food had rice hulls added to it to bulk it up and add roughage. Rice hulls are used as a growing medium in commercial mushroom production. This ingredient coupled with Heidi's eating of the mushroom growing kit's contents might have changed Heidi's digestive system. But one thing was absolutely certain. The dog food changed Heidi's poop. It was now a fungus-friendly host for spores.

She picked up her phone and called Carl.

"Hey, Carl," said Julie. "Have a minute for a short walk outside?"

"Sure. Right now?" Carl asked.

"Yep, right now," Julie replied. "See you at the sphere."

"What's up?" Carl asked when they approached each other. "You sounded concerned and you look nervous."

"Remember that security breach when I raced home after Clark nearly cut off his finger?" she asked.

"Sure."

"You didn't see the whole report. I had a sample of one of our earlier batches in my lab coat as you know. What you don't know is that Heidi ate it. I now think it might have something to do with the CDC situation in Cleveland, but I can't figure it all out. I need your help."

"You mean we could be part of this?" Carl said with alarm.

Julie replied, "This is what I think could have happened. Several months ago I changed Heidi's dog food to one that contained rice hulls. The hulls are used for all kinds of commercial applications, but very commonly as fillers. They are also used as a growing medium in commercial mushroom production. The hulls do not get fully digested, pass through the body and are expelled in the stool. About the same time, Heidi ate the contents of my little 'Grow your own exotic mushroom kit.' Heidi knocked the kit on the floor and ate the shitakes, oysters, and other living mushrooms. This, coupled with the rice hull food, may have changed her system; I'm not sure. What I am sure about is that it changed her stool. Pardon the pun, particularly under the circumstances, but I think Heidi is now producing Holy Shit."

Carl replied, "This sounds like a real mess. If Heidi did eat the sample, and if it was fungal, and if it was active, then the sample's spores were probably not processed by the kidneys. Our top-secret fungus was then introduced into the wild and had the ideal medium to use as its host. It's possible. This is very fucked. But I can't see how it could have gotten to Cleveland."

"Carl," Julie said pointedly, "Clark took a road trip to Jackson Hole and met another family there. This was shortly after the incident. The other family also drove—from Pittsburgh. Clark took Heidi and the other family took their dog. Heidi could have contaminated the other dog or their stools could have blended or shared elements somehow. Remember, we'd been bombarding these hybrids with 7.83 Hz for weeks. Who knows what we did to them. Then on the drive home, the other family could have stopped in Cleveland, I suppose. I'm now guessing that Clark drove the fungi halfway across the country, with Heidi doing her business all along the way. The other family then drove it in the other direction."

"Julie," Carl said, "you need to let Paulo know. We don't want to get caught with our pants down."

"Oh, absolutely I need to let him know. The other thing you don't know is that the Chili King is on the scent. He seems to be putting some pieces of the puzzle together," Julie said.

"That," Carl said, "is not good news."

Rob, of course, was clueless about most of what had happened. He had no idea the dogshit 'shrooms were spreading all across the country as a result of Dr. Perthuis's husband, Clark, and their little road trip to Jackson Hole, Wyoming. Thanks to Heidi, the 'shrooms were now all across the Midwest. The Percivals' dog, Tuffy, had left an equally fertile trail of 'shrooms back to Pittsburgh, via Cleveland. Clark's friend from med school, and his family, had stopped to visit the Rock and Roll Museum in Cleveland. Tuffy had taken a dump on the side of the road. There now was a line of 'shrooms forming all along I-80 from San Francisco to Pittsburgh.

The 'shrooms were rapidly reproducing and being strewn

throughout the breadbasket. Trillions of spores were in the air. They were in and around several major cities, and cities with international airports, including Salt Lake City, Omaha, Jackson Hole, Chicago, and Pittsburgh. Since this fungus was so highly reproductive, and had both viral and bacterial properties, it would soon be everywhere. In Jackson Hole alone, there were enough rich guys from Europe, Asia and South America with their dogs to accelerate the global spread. The same could be said of other major cities. With foodstuffs and related agricultural products shipped worldwide each day, many originating in the breadbasket, this special doggie doody would be all over the globe in no time.

Rob had no idea what was really going on or what might happen now that the CDC was involved and the Associated Press newswire was onto the story. He might get screwed, but the shit was literally going to hit the fan. A global event was about to unfold, and Rob had unwittingly played an important role.

I kind of started this whole thing, he thought proudly. He felt powerful because he believed he was the only person who really knew the whole story. Little did Rob know that he was but one actor, albeit an important one, on a much larger stage with many more players.

Fortunately for everyone, particularly the good guys, at least 40,000 people had an empirical understanding about what "toxic and dangerous" actually meant. In their eyes, the story in the press was complete bullshit. And 40,000 was a really good start, in the age of instant, uncontrollable, and unrestrained digital communication. It is not really possible to put the lid on what was soon to be millions of high school and college kids tweeting and friending each other. There would soon be two groups or classes of people, those who knew the 'shrooms provided a really great trip and those who bought into the government's fear-mongering propaganda.

Chapter Twenty-Three

'S hroom-spotting, as it was now referred to in the media, was starting to become worldwide activity. The little dogshit 'shrooms were being spotted on most other continents. It was concentrated around the large cities, but the spotting quickly spread, first into suburban and then into rural areas. The blogosphere, social networks, and tweets were growing along with the actual "'shroomspread." The trippy tweeters introduced this term. It was all about *the 'shroomspread*. People were picking them off dog poop and eating them all over the world. It was like Haight-Ashbury in 1966, but now it was instantly global. Use and awareness, and the 'shrooms themselves, were expanding at exponential rates, with timeframes compressing at equally fast rates.

The world's people were beginning to trip out and the governments were beginning to flip out. Mainstream news coverage was replete with warnings about toxicity and overdoses, and long-term damage to the liver. The official stories took great care to imply that the 'shrooms would be linked to birth defects. There was no empirical evidence to that effect, but they had floated the same sort of nonscience in the sixties about LSD, with about as much success. As a last resort, Art Linkletter was even cinema-graphically exhumed to retell the tragic story of his daughter leaping out of a building because of LSD. It was a remarkable propaganda effort. The phrase biological terrorism was invoked and it didn't play very well. The people from the sixties smelled the nonsense. Lots of youth actually knew how great the little doggie dynamite was. What was happening made class warfare look like child's play. This was a war of awareness; a war between those who actually understood the truth through direct personal experience and those who had no experience or understanding, but had great power. It was Galileo and the Church on steroids.

The government was telling the people to carefully "moni-tor" their dogs and to take any "toxic mushrooms" they found, put them in paper bags and microwave them for 5 minutes. This would kill the "toxic agents." Some government leaders proposed "disposing of all the dogs." After surprisingly serious debate, it was concluded that this would be political suicide and almost cer-tainly trigger civil disobedience. What were they going to do, kill all of man's best friends?

What no one knew was that the hybrid strain of SREP-SPG-19-S-31, the one that Heidi had eaten and Clark had helped deposit all over America, and in turn the globe, had not stopped evolving.

In addition to being flown and driven all over the world by travellers, SREPSPG-19-S-31 also migrated on its own, organi-cally. Spores traveled easily by air. Within days, they were in every state in the union. When they reached the state of Oregon, how-ever, something truly remarkable happened. Talk about the law of unintended consequences; this was chaos theory at its most excit-ing. The largest living organism on earth, the fungus Armillaria ostoyae (AO), covering 2,384 acres, combined with SREPSPG-

19-S-31.

Small, genetically modified, hopped-up, psychoactive mushroom, meet giant mushroom. The two distinct mycelia molecularly bonded. This union was no mean freak of nature. Once the two mycelia combined, the "single organism" characteristic of AO genetically attached itself to SREPSPG-19-S-31. After the strains comingled, their new biological behavior mimicked an excitatory neurotransmitter. In fact, each cell in the mycelium now acted like a neurotransmitter. When one unit had received the chemical signal from its neighbouring cell, it passed the signal along to the next closest cell. This happened with a speed approaching that of firing synapses. SREPSPG-19-S-31-AO was fast and powerful. Within a few more days, or weeks at the outside, there would be one giant interconnected, highly psychoactive fungus covering all the landmasses of earth.

Only the range of host environments and the levels of life-sustaining elements—nutrients and water—limited its progress.

Chapter Twenty-Four

With the news out about Boardman, Ohio, the federal government reacted in a predictable manner, despite having only a superficial understanding of the fungal mutation's nature and its rapid growth and dispersion. After the local police and fire department made their assessments and attempted to assert control of the hazmat scene, the Centers for Disease Control arrived to develop risk assessments and plans to control and mitigate the identifiable risks. This work was being orchestrated out of the CDC's central office in Atlanta. The CDC had already been sent samples and was analyzing them in their Georgia laboratories. The samples they were analyzing, however, were at least a generation behind the newly mutated version that was spreading across the globe.

In situations with this much visibility, every organization with a political agenda and a budget inserted themselves in the mix. Each made an effort to take control and gain some kind of political or budgetary advantage. The Department of Homeland Security, the National Guard, the FBI, the CIA, the DEA, the US Marine Corps, the US Army, and the FCC were each vying for project control and leadership. The White House announced the formation of a fact-finding commission. It was the classic cluster-fuck over control and power.

The CDC gave all parties a very thorough briefing. The briefing covered disease, contagion, viral mutation, dispersion rates, and estimates on population impact by the hour, the day, the week and by the month. Among the items on the short list of key concerns was civil disobedience. If communications and containment were not managed very carefully, and the emotions of the populace kept front of mind, widespread panic was inevitable. Additional concerns were how to provide care for those who were contaminated and manifesting symptoms; approaches to eradicating the fungus; manpower requirements and, most significantly, the formal chain of command. Chain of command, or control of it, was being fought for on two fronts, operations and communications management. Never had communications management become so important. The meathead muscle tactics of the military were technically obsolete. This was a war progressing at the speed of thought.

The subject of communications management became a priority because there were two divergent messages being communicated. One was by the government and its agents. It was being delivered through traditional media, including Hound News and the major networks. The other information outlets were those of social media including Facebook, Twitter, blogs, rogue podcasters, and ham radio operators. These media channels were largely beyond the government's control, although desk jockeys at all of the agencies were assigned to monitor and track the chatter, an international message that the government did not like and considered dangerous. This freelance message was that the mushrooms were safe, fun, and the government was full of shit. The rogue communicators had taken a memorable line from Timothy Leary's playbook and slightly modified it. It now read, "Tune in and turn off TV." Everyone was in a situation with very fast moving elements with two distinct directions. Or so they thought. No one in a position of power or even those among the enthusiasts had any idea.

The CDC's recommendations were that the fungus needed to be analyzed in much greater detail and that a massive effort by the US government's military would 1) not help contain the spread and 2) inflame the population, because there were diametrically opposing opinions—and no actual proof—about what the fungus did and the nature of its threat to national security. The CDC further advised that the G8 nations be invited into the discussion because global contagion was virtually guaranteed.

Within days, the populations and the governments of the G8 nations were actively engaged in political and public dialogue. The populations of the G8 nations were ingesting the fungus along with the people of most other nations in the world. Predictably, among the world's leadership, there was contentious debate surrounding the manner in which the threat should be handled. In the Euro Zone, there was great competition between the French, Germans, and British as to which nation should head the taskforce. Although Germany was arguably the best country for the job, due to its well-structured army, well-oiled infrastructure, and strong currency, the memories of World War II were still too raw to give the Germans full control. The G8's debate on the rules of crisis management would continue for weeks; far too long and far too slow considering the speed with which the mushrooms had spread and the speed with which they were being consumed.

There was palpable tension, mutual resentment, and fear between the Chinese and the Japanese. The Chinese now had much more money and much more influence than the Japanese did. Their memories of each other's practices during World War II, however, still in living, lurid color, put each of them on edge. The Japanese were concerned that the Chinese would somehow figure out a way to finally get even with them for the many violations of human rights the Chinese believed they suffered at their hands. They, too, debated for weeks. The Middle East was in a complete free fall. The Latin American countries continued to argue about everything. No one cared at all about Africa.

Chapter Twenty-Five

The CDC's basic recommendation was that the fungus be viewed and managed from a public health perspective rather than from a military perspective. The CDC's project leader was announced with a large degree of fanfare. Their man at the helm was Dr. Jerold Lang, a graduate of MIT. Everyone called him Dr. Jerry. Dr. Jerry was a tall, sixtyish guy with a Harrison Ford sort of image. Dr. Jerry was in pretty good physical shape, clean-shaven, and wore a brown tweed sports coat and a denim shirt with a tie. He had a dry wit, a memory like a steel trap, and analytical brilliance. He also had a reputation for being brutally frank. His honesty had held him back in his career. He had been considered for very senior government positions, a Cabinet position at one point, and a Senate seat in another. In the end, however, the vetting groups concluded that he was his own man first and would not play ball in the interest of politics.

Although his audiences, bosses, and handlers often didn't like his conclusions—specifically his dispassionate and direct delivery of them and their implications—Dr. Jerry had never been wrong in his thirty-year tenure with the CDC. If you needed an unvarnished assessment of a disease, how to manage controlled substances, or what constitutes a public health risk, there was no one better and more respected than Dr. Jerry Lang. His recommendations weren't always followed, but in the post-mortem reviews of a given program's success or failure, the plans that failed were typically those that hadn't followed Dr. Jerry's advice. Those that succeeded had always followed his recommendations.

The first thing Dr. Jerry did after arriving on the scene was to have his team collect new samples of the fungus. These new samples were put on an F-16 and sent to Georgia to be analyzed with a fresh perspective. What they found was different, quite different, from the first samples they had analyzed. They were now reviewing SREPSPG-19-S-31-AO. Jerry and his team had never seen anything like SREPSPG-19-S-31-AO. They didn't know what it was, but decided to call it SREPS for short.

SREPS was a biologist's wet dream. It was a new life form. No one knew much about it except that it was new and multidimensional in its morphology, having bacterial, viral, and mycological reproductive properties. After analyzing its complex molecular structure, they quickly concluded that, unimpeded, the fungus would spread at a breathtaking speed. Since there was no identifiable starting point, to their knowledge, they couldn't go to the source. They resigned themselves to the conclusion that it would be on every major landmass within a few days, if not sooner, and then spread aggressively after that. It would spread biologically and more importantly, socially.

So much for trying to intelligently manage a situation. By the time Dr. Jerry and his team reached Cleveland, so had the all the other major units of the federal government. They had all heard the teleconference briefing by one of the CDC's senior researchers. Now, they were showing up in person and in large numbers. The military man in charge was three-star Army Brigadier General Andrew (Andy) William Curtain. General Curtain was a career military man, a graduate of West Point, and a veteran of all the major military actions from Vietnam on. He was trained in Special Forces and was a career soldier through and through. He loved his work and lived for crisis and combat. He was that rare commodity so prized by the government—born to fight, born to lead, didn't mind killing, and wasn't afraid to die.

He firmly believed that war was an integral and necessary part of man's evolution and a sociobiological mechanism for controlling population. He believed that the really important advances in technology were only made in times of war and conflict. He believed that all animal behavior was driven by fear and that it was this fear that propelled the human race forward. He was a Hegel man through and through.

At 5'10" and 180 pounds, he looked the part without an ounce of fat on his body. His square jaw, military haircut, and a five-inch scar going from his forehead to the middle of his left cheek, made him an imposing and intimidating person. He was tough as nails and didn't like taking no for an answer. As far as he was concerned, this was a military problem that needed the full force of the United States Armed Services to control. In General Curtain's view, this was just another enemy that needed to be exterminated. That enemy was not just SERPS, but also the dogs and people who ate them. General Curtain had a dangerously expansive view of this problem in his world. Curtain saw this as his World War III and he was its Douglas MacArthur.

He and Dr. Jerry were headed for a major pissing contest over who should be in control and more importantly what strategy should be used to manage the situation and control risk.

Chapter Twenty-Six

G eneral Curtain did what he had been well trained to do. He set up a command center and established a perimeter. The perimeter was greater Cleveland. Tanks and Army personnel carriers helped him cordon off the area. There were Harrier jets, MH-60 Black Hawk helicopters, Apache helicopters and C-130 Hercules transports at the Cleveland airport. General Curtain had the Apache helicopters fly over the area as much as possible to demonstrate that he was in command. All other air travel was now under his control and most of it he shut down. The National Guard was called into active duty and any Army, Navy, or Marine units that were not scheduled for deployment to Iraq, Afghanistan, or Iran were notified to be ready for active duty on domestic soil. The entire city was alive with armored personnel carriers, Hummers, and even a dozen or so Bradley tanks. There were planes and helicopters buzzing overhead and uniformed troops everywhere. All of the troops and the CDC task force members wore protective air filter masks. The city of Cleveland was now, technically, a war zone.

Much of the population was frightened, confused, and increasing bifurcated. The news channels were now covering this event exclusively, not just in Cleveland, but also everywhere in the US. Increasingly the "mushroom threat" was being covered around the globe. In Cleveland, a nine p.m. curfew was put into place and people were instructed to take extra precautions with their food, water and, in particular, their dogs. They were told that if they found SREPS, to collect the samples and to make sure to wear rubber gloves. The instructions to put any found mushrooms in a paper bag and microwave them for three minutes was repeated every half hour.

General Curtain commanded his troops to halt all ground traffic in and out of the area and sent his troops on a search and destroy mission. The troops were armed with herbicides and flamethrowers. They went street by street. General Curtain quickly did the arithmetic in his head. With the country's military already stretched thin in two and a half active wars and hundreds of thousands of troops stationed in 168 countries around the world, there was no way this problem, his problem, could be adequately handled with ground forces. Cleveland was but one small dot on the US map, and it had already consumed ten percent of the available US-based military resources. He acknowledged to himself that his efforts were futile. He was not, however, going to relinquish his power to some egghead from the CDC.

General Andy needed air power and broader authority to eradicate this new threat to national security. He speculated that the country was under attack from insurgent terrorists and that biological weapons were the enemy's tools of choice. He couldn't exactly identify the enemy, but that would be for someone in the communications area to do. Maybe blame it on al Qaeda or even Castro and the communists. He thought that perhaps Castro was working with Venezuela's Chavez, and in concert with the Chinese or North Koreans. General Curtain had always wanted to blow that fucking island of Cuba off the map anyway and this was as good a chance as he was going to get.

Scientists and the military get along really well when they are working together to design and develop weapons. They have a common purpose and the time and money to help all parties feel good, get the job done and then get adequately rewarded. The C-130 transport, the Sherman tank, the Apache helicopter, and the A-bomb were good examples of excellent collaborative work between the military and the propeller heads from the scientific community. Regardless of one's feelings about war and mass destruction, these were well-designed, well-produced, highly effective pieces of equipment. Scientists and military leaders don't, however, work very well together in times of crisis. They get along even worse if there are management and control issues that require quick resolution.

Generally, the military likes to shoot first and ask questions later. If there is collateral damage, the military's position is that there would have been some regardless of the plan. Military personnel accept the harsh reality that war is tough and that people die or get their legs blown off. Death and injury are unavoidable and inevitable. If you are not man enough to buy into this psychology, get out of the way and let the real men handle things. These real soldiers would be thanked later.

Scientists, on the other hand, are by definition measured thinkers. They are trained to observe. They are trained to look for patterns. They are interested in the truth behind questions and the answers. They want to make sure that what they are observing is actually what it appears to be, not an artifact of an episodic condition. Scientists search for reason and logic. They search for reliability. When these two divergent points of view are placed together and tasked with crisis management, an unbridgeable philosophical chasm always emerges.

In addressing the large issue of general management and approach, process, logic, and reason are useless tools in resolving these great differences in perspective. Trying to arrive at a consensus between these two groups in a rational way is pointless. Why? Because the military personnel are generally bigger, more aggressive, tougher, and better armed. They typically win the argument. If they didn't win the argument, they would simply kill or lock up their opposition. The pen may be mightier than the sword, but only in the two-dimensional, higher-order-thinking world. Add the third, sweaty, blood-soaked dimension, and it is always safer to bet on the heavy artillery. This was certainly the case in days of old. In current times, the military ultimately controls the technology and the weapons. If push comes to shove, the military will simply disable a communications network, reroute a plane, or in some manner marginalize their thoughtful opponents. The government's intervention in the movie ET is the classic contemporary example. The kids had it right, the government had it wrong. In the end, however, the forces of the good triumphed.

Chapter Twenty-Seven

D r. Jerry was beyond distressed at the plan the military was implementing. The only good news was that the military didn't have the resources to implement their offense. This would end up being just a lot of chest-pounding. The resource pools and geopolitical forces would force these grandiose ambitions into bureaucratic orbit. Dr. Jerry was much more stimulated by the discovery of a new life form. He was also heartened by the ineffectiveness of the government's media control and message-management efforts. Although the government and the news conglomerates had been frighteningly effective in dumbing down the population and limiting the dialogue to a handful of emotionally charged topics, they were very quickly losing their grip on the mushroom threat due to its very nature. More and more people were turning off their TVs. If they left them on, it was for the amusement of the news, not new information.

The old mass broadcasting tools were being replaced by new technologies. Once again, technology had migrated closer to the end-user. Today, anyone with a cell phone could become a force of change, delivering a message to millions. Dr. Jerry had seen what had happened in Egypt, Libya, Santiago, and even Madison, Wisconsin. The new media with YouTube, Facebook, and Twitter leading the pack were enabling political and social outcomes that were absolutely unimaginable just a few years ago.

Jerry suspected humankind was on the cusp of an event of biblical proportion, but he had no idea what it was. He was comforted in the knowledge that both SERPS and the firsthand communication of its effects were each moving at such remarkably fast rates that the military could plan whatever it wanted. As committed as they might be, they would never have enough time to launch their plans; or even to really plan, for that matter. Being a researcher at heart, however, he simply wanted to learn much more about the make-up of this SERPS life form. This was a once-in-a-lifetime opportunity.

As Dr. Jerry considered his pool of resources, HGMP came to mind. They were tinkering with new genetic variations, were leaders in biodiversity and Julie, his old acquaintance from MIT, was there. He put in a call to HGMP to see if he could get her input. Surprisingly, she did not return his call. Jerry considered this odd since they had always been on very good terms.

Unbeknownst to Jerry, Julie was briefing Paulo as Jerry's call came in. She saw his name on her iPhone screen.

As Julie sat in Paulo's office looking out over the campus, she said, "Paulo, I think we have a problem. I believe, and so does Carl, that the toxic mushroom outbreak in Cleveland is a direct by-product of our 4.20 project. What we think happened is that, as you'll recall, my dog ate our sample. We believe the kidneys did not process the active psychotropic agent. The sample then found the canine stool to be a viable reproductive medium. Around that same time, my husband took our family, including our dog, on a road trip to Wyoming. While there, they met another family who also brought along their dog. We believe there was some sort of contamination between the two dogs. Then the other dog dropped her stool, along with the spores, in and around Cleveland and presumably, other places along their route back to Pittsburgh. I believe it won't be long until this circles back to us. We should start thinking about damage control."

"So this is just one more unlucky break for Cleveland." Paulo looked out the window for a moment and then turned to look at Julie. "Who else knows this theory other than the three of us?"

"Cleveland is utterly beside the point. This is everywhere. As far as I know, no one else knows. I did receive an odd call from Professor Earp about two hours ago. He suspects something and was poking around, but I didn't give him any new information."

"Let's each think about this for a few hours and then you, Carl, and I should meet and compare notes. I don't want this blowing up in our hands."

"And what about T Mike? I'm hoping this has diverted his attention for the moment, but I can't believe he's lost interest. Can he not have put this together by now?" Paulo's cell phone went off. He looked at the number and then said to Julie, "Please stick around. We better get our act together and quickly. This is the White House and I suspect it's not just a social call."

Dr. Jerry, after not hearing back from Julie, and operating in a real-time crisis-management mode, had someone from the White House call Verdoccia. Jerry needed answers and didn't have the luxury of time to wait for Julie. The message from the White House, or more accurately their order, was to call Jerry Lang immediately. Paulo placed the call immediately and Julie listened.

"Dr. Lang, this is Paulo Verdoccia, with HGMP. I was asked to give you a call. How are you?"

"Hello, Paulo," replied Lang. "Fine, thanks. I tried calling Julie

Perthuis, but couldn't reach her. Sorry to bother you, but we're under the gun here."

"I completely understand." Paulo rolled his eyes at Julie. "As chance would have it, Julie's here with me now. Should I put this call on speaker?"

"Good idea."

"Hello, Jerry," said Julie. "Sorry I missed your call earlier."

"No problem. It's worked out for the better since I now have both of you on the line. As I'm sure you're aware, we've got quite a situation on our hands in Cleveland. The CDC's view of the situation is that this mushroom that's now captured the world's attention is a new life form. It doesn't match anything we've ever examined. We need some help in classifying it."

Paulo said, "Yes, we've seen the news. In fact, Julie and I were just discussing how backlogged we are and that this is something we would normally love to be involved in, but we're stretched with other national defense work."

Dr. Jerry couldn't believe what he was hearing. "Dr. Verdoccia, you've seen the news? Don't you realize we have a potentially explosive situation unfolding? The prospect of widespread civil disobedience is becoming increasingly real and we'd like you to spring free a few people to help us sort this out before it is too late. What's the problem?" Lang didn't bother trying to hide his growing anger and frustration. "Look, let's at least get your help on a biological match to see if this strain resembles anything you've seen. You should have some databases we don't have. Let's just see if you get a match—even a partial."

Paulo sighed. "My hands are tied, Dr. Lang."

Julie shrugged at Paulo and started to speak. "Maybe I can find—"

"That would be a great help to us and not excessively time-consuming. And Dr. Verdoccia, this is a big, heavy, fast-moving train. I'd get on board rather than run the risk of being hit by it," Lang finished with an aggressive and authoritative tone.

Paulo really didn't have a good defense to this relatively simple request, so he relented and said, "Okay, Jerry. I'll spring Julie loose and see what we come up with."

"I need this turned around yesterday. There is no time to spare. I'll have some samples to you in a couple of hours and need a quick analysis by tomorrow morning. I am legally required to tell you this is a national security project and therefore needs to be treated with the utmost confidentiality." Lang sounded smug.

"Understood. I'm glad we can help," said Paulo.

Jerry thanked him for his willingness to help, but was really pissed off at Verdoccia's attitude. Jerry was now also suspicious. He thought, *No research organization on the planet would turn down an offer to help on a project of this scope and significance.* He smelled a rat.

Dr. Jerry told Paulo that he'd put a sample and the CDC's preliminary review on an F-14 and HGMP would have it in two hours. With this unexpected and weird reaction from HGMP, Jerry also concluded he needed a second opinion. Since HGMP was now suspect as a reviewer, Jerry decided to call the oracle of taxonomy and the world's leading expert in psychomycology, Dr. Wyatt Earp. Jerry and Wyatt knew each other through their research papers and through participating and presenting at various conferences over the years. They weren't friends, but good acquaintances.

Jerry found Earp's number in his cell phone and hit it.

"Dr. Earp, Jerry Lang here. How are things?" Jerry asked.

"I am doing just fine. Thanks so much for asking, but you tell me. I've been expecting your call." Earp replied without missing a beat. "Sounds as if you've got a live one on your hands. With all of this Myco-excite in the streets, I figured it was just a matter of time until you guys would need to pick my brain. I'm sure you're in the middle of a political and public relations shitstorm. I'm all ears. It's your nickel."

"I'd say so," replied Jerry. "I need your help. We indeed have a mycological anomaly on our hands, or as we say at the CDC, 'we don't know what the fuck this is.'"

"Yes, that's the same professional jargon we use in academia," Earp said dryly.

Jerry explained the little he knew, that the fungal life form was, as far as they could tell, a new and unclassified fungus, that it was powerful and spreading fast. He needed a fresh set of eyes to review what the CDC knew so far and asked if he could send over some samples for Earp's analysis. He also asked if Earp would review a confidential report written by the folks at HGMP. Earp's antenna went up at the mention of HGMP. HGMP had their fingers in too many things and HGMP's proximity to the sample Earp had received from Sally's dog walker buddy, suddenly took on new significance for him.

Earp laughed and replied, "Send it over. We'd be happy to put her through the paces. Fortunately for you, I was planning to leave for Peru in a couple of days, so your call was well timed. But I'll postpone my trip if I need to so I can help you and our government. You know how much I respect their moral imperatives and their religious imperialism, all nicely packaged under their Doctrine of Pre-emption. In all seriousness though, Jerry, this area of mycology is of great personal interest to me, as you know, as is the task of its taxonomy. Please send over what you have and I will get back to you as quickly as I can. Just so you are aware, and in the interest of full disclosure, I'll restrict my team to just two people, my research assistant and me. Is it safe to assume I have no budgetary constraints and should bill you directly at the CDC?"

Jerry said, "Absolutely, Wyatt, the last thing anyone cares about at this stage is money."

"Great," Earp said, his eyes alight at the dual gift of a new challenge and free financial rein.

"It will be there in a couple of hours along with the CDC's preliminary findings. In the interest of my full disclosure, this is a National Security project, so secrecy is required. Keep your circle small."

"Understood," Earp said.

Jerry hung up.

Unbeknownst to Jerry, Earp was already a couple of steps ahead of the CDC. After he and Sally had run their initial analyses and received a verbal report from Rob that he had eaten the 'shrooms and not died, both Sally and Earp also had eaten some of the 'shrooms themselves. Earp and Sally were each devout acrophiles. They loved getting high and specifically loved the psychedelic end of the drug spectrum. Even within their extremely wide and deep range of hallucinogenic experiences, this new stuff was in its own class. It was not just powerful. It was not just otherworldly. Significantly, it gave Sally and Earp the true sense of a shared consciousness. It was, at times during their experimentation, like being cognitive Siamese twins. They were of one mind. Earp and Sally took as many notes as they could while they were tripping until it became impossible to do so. They had a pretty good understanding of what this stuff was when it started. They weren't sure what is was now and Earp was anxious to not only analyze its chemical composition and morphology, but to try some of the new stuff and see what if any changes had occurred relative to its onset, efficacy, and duration of effects. Earp laughed to himself that he actually got paid to do what he did. He'd send the CDC a whopper of an invoice for this work.

When the samples and write-up arrived at HGMP, Paulo called in Julie and Carl for a quick meeting. He told them they had been more or less forced into helping out a bit.

"Again," muttered Julie.

He proudly said that he had been able to limit their involvement, but the White House was involved and he had to at least appear cooperative. Paulo realized that if he didn't help, he would be getting more help than he wanted without asking for it. The prospect of a team of forensic data analysts pulling up in five government-issue black Suburbans was a scenario he wanted to avoid at all costs.

He instructed Carl and Julie to read the CDC report and to also run a comparative analysis to see if the CDC sample matched anything in their databases. Paulo told them to get it done immediately.

"I don't want to get dragged into this any more than we've been already, so wrap it completely by eight a.m. so we can get this back to the CDC and with a bit of luck, move on. Let's meet later today and see what we've got to work with," he said.

Chapter Twenty-Eight

J ulie was charged with running the tests. She, Carl, and Paulo each read the CDC report. They each had similar thoughts, suspicions, and fears, but no one said anything. When the test results came back they found that the CDC sample matched SREPSPG-19-S-31, but with a few odd and dangerous add-ons, particularly the mushroom from Oregon. They now knew they had a Really Big Problem, literally and figuratively. The sample they reviewed was a variant of the strain that Julie had accidentally taken out of the building when her husband Clark had sliced off part of his finger. There was no doubt about it. This was the strain that was connected with Julie's well-documented violation of HGMP security protocol. This was the strain that was part of T. Mike's top-secret project. They were all in a really tough spot with one foot on the boat and the other on the dock. They had one foot on the side of truth and science and the other on the side of war, politics, and propaganda. They were fucked, and not sure which way it would go.

While Julie and Carl were trying to figure out what to do, the United States government and leaders of other important nations were grappling with their options, and the young people of the world were partying their asses off. For all intents and purposes, every college campus in America, and now increasingly around the rest of the world, was closed. They were closed at least as far as teaching went. Otherwise, they had never been more vibrant. It was tripomania; it was tripomania everywhere. This was the uber-party of all uber-parties. The local police departments had simply given up. There was music blasting everywhere. It was booming out of dorm and frat house windows. Deadmou5 was never more alive. There were rock bands playing in the streets. Kids were painting their faces and wearing flowers. There was nothing funny about peace, love, and understanding now. They were turned on and tuned in. It was the zeitgeist.

Carl called for a meeting with Julie and Paulo in the form of a stroll around campus. When they were outside, Paulo tried to break the ice by commenting on the brilliant three quarter moon in the sky.

Julie wasn't interested in bullshit and started the real conversation. "Let's not beat around the bush. I think we all know exactly what happened. My dog Heidi ate my homework a couple of months ago. That fungus sample appears to have somehow morphed and I'm pretty sure now that's how the whole thing started. It started here started by growing on Heidi's shit. Go fucking figure! Then it seems to have spread like a bad rumor. Then, it morphed again. This thing has in it much of what we are developing for 4.20, but it's now part virus and part bacterium. On top of that, it is arguably the largest organism on the planet after hooking-up with that strain in Oregon. The CDC report specifically references that fungal strain.

"At the moment, I do not see any solution to containing it. Based on my off-the-cuff forecast, we're going to have many hundreds of millions of people tripping their asses off within a few weeks, if not days. Just look at what's going on down the road on campus. It's like the entire town is at a giant Dead concert. If I weren't seeing and hearing it with my own eyes and ears, I wouldn't believe it."

Carl said that he thought there was an ethical obligation, and certainly a fiduciary responsibility, to be straight foreword in communicating to their Board of Directors, T Mike, and perhaps the White House, what had happened. He said at least at that point, we have come clean and will not be subject to punitive or aggressive legal action. He thought they could at least preserve their reputations.

Everyone at HGMP had absolutely known that it was simply a matter of time before fooling with Mother Nature would have some kind of serious unintended consequence. Now they really had one.

Paulo jumped in, "Maybe there is some middle ground to consider. We could render a report and not disclose exactly what happened, but offer a hypothesis and simply remain oblique about some of the details. Technically, we cannot discuss any of the details anyway or we will violate our confidentiality agreement with Bellihurton. That would ignite the ire—to put it mildly—of Homeland Security. We could each be locked up for decades be-cause they would likely apply antiterrorism laws and treat us as enemy combatants. I think we need to be very careful about doing the right thing with a full disclosure. This could be one of those good deeds that would absolutely receive severe punishment."

They were quiet for a minute or so, which is a long time when there is a heavy subject and a big decision in the air.

Finally, Julie said, "I think Paulo is right. Considering the people who got us started on this, we would all get completely screwed if this got tied back to project 4.20 and its funding. The company would be dismantled or discredited. All of our government contracts would be cancelled. We would all certainly be sent to federal prison for a long time, and there would be no getting out on appeal. The laws of normal jurisprudence do not apply to enemy combatants. As they say in South America, we would be 'disappeared,' and quickly."

Julie decided to do the write-up. She stuck to the facts. Explained the taxonomy as well as possible. She explained the potency of the psychoactive chemicals. She explained not only the vastness of this new organism, but also the possibility that simultaneous users might actually have shared perceptions of specific events and surroundings. Julie hypothesized, toward the end of her report, that the organism likely manifested itself in one animal and/or its feces, and then it simply spread. The first host animal could have been a dog, or the strain could have jumped species. This was one of the theories about the origin and spread of the AIDS virus; that it began in lower primates and spread to humans. She further speculated that the fungus could also be an unforeseen by-product of genetically modified vegetables.

In concluding her report, Julie noted that at least there were no deaths or diseases resulting from this outbreak, but that it could have a significant impact on general awareness, attitudes, and opinions.

The report was about fifteen pages of narrative with six tables and charts, each covering some part of the taxonomy, the elements, chemical compounds, and their concentrations. Julie concluded that she didn't believe that HGMP could be of any more assistance, but that the company had been honored and privileged to be of whatever help they had been in the interest of helping manage a national security issue. Paulo and Carl read it, made a few minor changes and signed off on its content. They then sent the highly encrypted report to Dr. Jerry through a secure network.

Chapter Twenty-Nine

An hour and a half after Lang's conversation with Earp, a trio of uniformed Air Force personnel arrived at Earp's office. *Fuck, these guys are fast. I guess it pays to use the Air Force as your courier service providers*, Earp thought. *Gives new meaning to the word FedEx.*

One of the enlisted men had a metal briefcase handcuffed to his wrist. The soldiers presented their identification papers and a letter from Dr. Jerry. The soldiers then asked Dr. Earp for his picture identification and had him sign for the receipt of the briefcase's contents. The contents were in aluminum cylinders, labelled SERPS and dated with the current day's date. The soldiers then walked to their US Air Force helicopters and flew away. They had done the same routine at HGMP a half an hour earlier.

Earp walked over to the to far side of his office, took a seat in his 1920s-era brown leather club chair and put his feet up on the ottoman. He clasped his fingers and put them behind his head and began to think about the events converging upon him.

Earp's office was a sight to behold. It contained thirty odd years of photographs, some with dignitaries, some with US presidents, photos of himself with the last three presidents of Peru, curios and objects of art from his many travels around the world. One wall was adorned in its entirety with academic degrees, certificates of achievement and awards from world-renowned organizations including the National Geographic Society, the American Academy of Sciences, the National Institutes of Health and the American Medical Association. Looking over the documents and the photos one was overwhelmed with the length and significance of Earp's career, his achievements, and his stature in the world of serious thought.

In addition to the commemorative appointments, there were hundreds of books, journals and magazines in various languages. There were jars of plant and animal specimens and at least twenty stacks of files, work papers, and assorted items in print.

Earp's large wooden desk was a leftover from America's postwar period of mass institutionalization. It was a mammoth mahogany statement of authority and had probably come from a courthouse or government office, as did his large eight-by-three-foot walnut worktable. The surfaces were so cluttered it was difficult to see the desk's top. The worktable was the same; virtually covered from end to end with piles of work. Despite the incredible clutter and apparent disorganization, Earp knew exactly where everything was located in his office. His mind would click into a subject area and he'd react with a jolt and walk to a seemingly random stack, finger his way to a certain depth, and then pull out the precise document he needed for a reference or for continued work.

Earp had a ménage of computer gear, including a few relics, among them the NeXT and a 512 Mac. He also had the latest stuff from Apple. On the wall, he had a 60-inch LED monitor so he could review materials from either his desk or his reading chair.

As Earp started thinking, he went back to the night he received the e-mail from Sally. He knew at the time there was something big and odd going on with the sample Sally had gotten from her friend. He suspected then, and even more so now, that the government or some powerful organization was behind it. Now, with the mention of HGMP, coupled with Air Force couriers and the CDC, he was convinced his suspicions were well grounded. All of this was against the backdrop of the 'shroomorama occurring all around them. From what Earp could tell, a meaningful segment of the world's population was tripping. *That's a huge deal.*

He pulled his iPhone from his pocket, went to the recent calls list and pressed Sally's name and number.

Sally answered, "Hi, Professor. What do you need?"

"We need to take a little trip. What's your schedule?"

"I'm pretty much free for the next three days. I have some papers to review and some tests to run, but nothing that can't be moved around," Sally replied.

"Well," Earp said, "Please pack an overnight bag and come over to my office as soon as you can. I'll fill you in when you get here."

When Sally arrived, Earp was lost in thought, reading the reports that had just been delivered. He was relaxing in his large leather chair.

She said, "What do you make of the world party?"

Earp replied with a tone of seriousness and considerable reflection, "I'm not sure yet."

"Where are we going?"

"We'll know when we get there," said Earp cryptically.

"Take a look in the aluminum cylinders on the coffee table."

Sally picked up the cylinders with "Property of the US Centers for Disease Control" etched onto their surfaces.

Earp said, "These are the latest samples of the mushrooms. The CDC had the Air Force deliver them, with the aid of an F-16, about an hour ago. I've been asked to review their report and to provide an independent analysis. I've also been asked to review HGMP's report, which I expect to receive tomorrow. I've told the CDC that you would also be working on the project. The trip we'll be taking will occur in this room with the aid of whatever is in those cylinders."

"Wow," Sally said. "Do you think HGMP is involved?"

"I don't know," said Earp, "But I had the same reaction. So, let's do this. Let's run our analyses and get a better understanding of what we're about to eat. From what I've read—the reports are on the desk, by the way—these 'shrooms are related to the sample you got from your old friend, the dog-walker. Now it's starting to sound *really* interesting, don't you think? This generation, however, has morphed significantly from its parent or whatever it was when we reviewed and tested it a few months ago. This strain appears to be stronger, more potent. And it has mutated. It now appears to have viral and bacterial properties in addition to those of a fungus. That is to say, it has a three dimensional reproductive system. It has also apparently mated with Armillaria ostoyae."

Sally's eyes widened with both wonder and alarm.

"That could mean this sample on the desk is just a cutting from one very, very large 'shroom," Sally said insightfully and with considerable awe.

"Precisely. I think this is more than just a new ballgame. I think this is a whole new sport. Let's get the lab work out of the way and then see what this shit actually does."

Sally and Earp read the CDC report and then spent about six hours in the lab, working until the wee hours of the morning.

They crashed in Earp's office and got three hours of sleep. Sally slept on Earp's couch and Earp slept in his big comfy office chair with his feet stretched out over the ottoman. In the morning, after the computers spat out the results, their analyses confirmed the first of Earp's three main theories.

There would be no stopping this fungus. It was more robust and biologically resilient than anything either of them had ever analyzed in their careers. In addition, since it had acquired viral and bacterial properties, there were no known agents to kill it or impede its spread. Anything that could conceivably kill it, such as radioactivity or a variation of extreme chemotherapy, would kill everything near it. Since SERPS was approaching a saturation point of full coverage on the earth's fertile land surfaces, eradicating it would lead to eradicating all of the earth's land-based food sources and the ground used to support them.

Around ten a.m. Earp received an encrypted communication for Jerry Lang. It contained a copy of the HGMP report, authored by Dr. Julie Perthuis. This confirmed Earp's second theory: that HGMP was much more involved than he had been led to believe by Jerry Lang, and more to the point, by Julie. Earp was also now pretty certain that Lang did not have the full story from HGMP either. Lang was just a CDC guy after all. A good guy and a smart guy, but after you cut through all the bullshit, he was a government bureaucrat. Earp had written many scientific papers and been on many review panels, as had Lang. But Earp was street smart and not just regular street smart; he'd been lost and found on the cosmic sidewalks too. He knew bullshit when he read it. As cleverly written as the HGMP report was, key pieces of thought and fairly obvious logical extensions of their research findings were conspicuously absent. Why were they left out? HGMP was hiding something. Earp was absolutely certain of it.

Earp was also certain that if he poked around for answers in the wrong manner, he and Sally could end up getting tossed out of an airplane over the Pacific Ocean. There was another piece to this puzzle and Earp wasn't sure he wanted to be the one to disclose it.

Earp's third theory was that this new psychoactive toy was going to make the first empirical data that he and Sally gathered look like a mild cup of tea. They had to get their administrative chores out of the way first; write the report on their finding and opine on the HGMP report. Then, off to the wild blue yonder.

Chapter Thirty

When Dr. Jerry read HGMP's report, he found the comments toward the end to be the most interesting, *"that there could be significant changes in perceptions, attitudes, and opinions and that this strain did not appear to cause disease or death."* The report clearly tried to dampen the perceived threat that had come to surround this outbreak. Lang needed to put together a press conference and quickly. Everyone from the president to the man in the street was getting really uncomfortable. This was an increasingly global problem and consequently information management, from one person's or one government's perspective, was not going to be possible.

When the press conference began, Dr. Jerry told the reporters that the government had launched the largest analysis and containment effort in US history. He stated emphatically that there had been no reported deaths and that the strain did not appear to be linked to any known diseases. He also mentioned that in the opinion of one of the country's most esteemed research institutes, HGMP, the strain was probably started in one host animal, in all likelihood a canine. Then, after the strain stabilized within its host, it quickly morphed and spread. Dr. Jerry noted that they did not have any leads on the original source of the fungus, but they were working diligently and as quickly as possible to identify the original source. Then, he opened the session up for questions. He urged caution and control for the citizenry and the various branches of law enforcement. His parting thought was for everyone to try and relax and behave as normal, but heed the curfew. Jerry explained that the curfew was temporary, imposed only to reduce the level of general activity and give the authorities the opportunity for more focus and more efficient manpower utilization. He concluded by saying the best minds in the field were going to solve the questions of the mushroom's source, efficacy, potential, and risks.

Chapter Thirty-One

Rob the dog-walker was watching TV and when he realized what he had actually heard, he quickly put two big pieces of the puzzle together. He said to himself, you've gotta be fucking shitting me, she started all of this. Rob knew that Mrs. Perthuis worked for HGMP. It was easy for Rob to keep Julie Perthuis in mind because she was really hot. Rob had occasionally fantasized about her.

Right now, he was fantasizing about what to do with the information he had just put together. He could go to Julie and tell her that he had figured it all out and was the first person to eat the mushrooms. He could go to HGMP and tell them. He could go to the press and make a big splash. He could go to the government or the CDC. If there ever was a time to smoke a bowl and take a long reflective walk, this was it. Rob fired up a little blaster and took a long walk. After thinking about all the options surrounding him making a disclosure, he concluded that nothing good could come from saying a word. There would only be ruin. He went through the outcomes in his mind.

Julie Perthuis' life would be ruined. HGMP would be ruined.

Heidi would be confiscated and probably dissected. He also reasoned that he would be arrested for something, just because... So, he decided to let sleeping dogs lie, as it were. This event should and would unfold on its own. It had already started to take on a life of its own and was very quickly becoming the biggest news item on the planet. There was no stopping the spread of information coming from all kinds of sources. The social networking tools were exploding with truth. Blogs were sprouting up almost as fast as the 'shrooms were spreading. There were blogs about how fucked-up the governments were. There were blogs about conspiracy theories, that the world was experiencing its End of Days, that the 'shrooms were forms of extraterrestrial life, that this was another government attempt to control by fear. The religious right in the US was having a field day complaining about the shortcomings of government crisis management, speculating on what Jesus would do, and of course, asking for even bigger financial donations during this period of unprecedented need. You name it, someone was writing about it.

This was happening in countries that very much disliked enlightened points of view: China, Iran, Iraq, Israel, Venezuela, Nigeria, North Korea, South Africa, the US, and Russia, to name a few. It was global. It was viral. It was powerful. The overwhelming number of personal, individual messages came from *the experienced*. These messages came from those who had tried the 'shrooms. Their comments were positive and came from all walks of life and all socioeconomic groups. Everyone was represented in the mix. Even members of the police, the military, and politicians were weighing in on the side of the Good. They were singing high praise and the singing got louder and more harmonious by the day, if not by the hour. The spread of the 'shrooms was extensive. Just walk outside, look down and spot one. Couldn't be easier.

And they were free. Lots of people were trying them.

When these people came down and their trips ended, they wrote about their transcendent experiences. Almost without exception, they recommended that everyone should try them. More and more people did. This was becoming an event of biblical proportions. Rob was starting to believe that this could actually change the world. As far as he was concerned, however, his role in it was over. He was going to keep his head down, his eyes and ears open, and his shoulder to the grindstone. The last thing Rob wanted was scrutiny. He did have, after all, a half million bucks in cash buried in his mother's garden and he could never concoct an audit trail to satisfy even the dumbest IRS investigator. No, this was the time to sit back and watch the world go by.

Chapter Thirty-Two

W hile the scientists, Army guys, and politicians were arguing about what to do, more and more of the world's people were tripping, and in turn, becoming increasingly suspicious about the news they were reading and hearing. Once someone actually tried the 'shrooms, they knew the truth. In vast numbers, they joined the other experienced people and became vocal opponents to the fear-mongerers. This phenomenon was now much bigger than a movement. It was a global sea change in awareness and consciousness. It was growing organically, without a leader, and getting larger by the hour. All under the gaze of the watchful and thoughtful John Galt.

Everett, Pennsylvania was largely a town unknown. It was located in south central Pennsylvania and was supported by the small farms in its surrounding areas and a few small businesses. It was an attractive little rural town with well-maintained buildings from the late 1800s and a rich history dating back to the period in America when the indigenous peoples considered this their home. It was also important during the Civil War. Being close to the Mason-Dixon line, the area received a lot of political and military traffic and its related commerce. Everett was also less than two hundred miles from Washington DC.

Today, Everett was a town forsaken, a town that no one cared about anymore. It was an artifact of days gone by, when life was simple and gasoline was thirty-five cents a gallon. Today, however, its population was small and shrinking, people were poor, their political views were conservative, and their educational system mirrored that of the rest of the county; it was underfunded, deteriorating, and ineffective. The population didn't know much and cared even less about learning more. Everett was a good town if you wanted to blend in and get lost from the rest of the world. This is just what John had done, albeit with a purpose and commitment to a cause much larger than the little town of Everett.

This quaint little town was home to the charming Union Hotel, in which George Washington had stayed on one of his trips from Washington, DC. It had history and character, but was now a destination spot for young rednecks to drink beer, watch Steelers' football games, complain about the incompetence of big government, and spout off about the need to "take back our country." None of these rednecks was quite sure from whom they were taking back their country, nor what they would do with it were they to succeed, but it was an easy theme to glom on to and gave the barflies an easy and recurring subject to bitch about.

The Union Hotel was also the temporary residence of John Galt, mild-mannered computer tech sent to help the Everett Savings and Loan upgrade their old software and network systems so they could comply more easily with the new rules governing loans backed by the federal government. John chose to live in the Union because his workload was heavy, he didn't have the time or interest to shop, cook, clean, or do any household-related chores. The hotel was perfect because their kitchen and service were good, and he could slither into a social scene easily by buying a few beers when the Steelers, Penguins, or Pirates played and of course, by going to church on Sunday. John could talk the talk, complain about the government, and buy an occasional round for the many patrons receiving unemployment compensation or permanent disability.

John had crafted an easy manner and a benign, nondescript image. He wore nice clothes from Wal-Mart. Since the people in the town were largely uneducated, not one person had made a joke about his name. Because John worked for the local bank, the townspeople welcomed his presence and were very helpful in getting John properly set-up in the Union Hotel, technologically speaking anyway.

John had a dedicated T1 line that bypassed the hotel's system and paralleled the network infrastructure of the Savings and Loan. Once that was in place, John had a fully route-redundant and route-diverse network in place. He could anonymously e-mail anywhere in the world without a trace back to him. Except for the last mile into Everett, John's network could survive a national catastrophe. John had a powerful side job with a global social network called Wikileaks. This was where John focused his important attention. The bank jobs and other similar assignments were simply good cover so he could pursue his other, much more important, interests.

Wikileaks' mission was to find the truth and then tell the truth to the world, regardless of whose truth it was and who might be adversely affected by it. They had almost a million followers and about a thousand people who did the kind of work John did. There was no one quite like John, though. The Wikileaks affiliates hacked into and then combed through the world's largest data banks. They extracted files, reports, communication logs, expense reimbursements, contracts between governments and paramilitary agents, personnel records—you name it, they looked for it. Anytime they found something that didn't support the official news story they leaked the real scoop. Anytime they found something that was intentionally hidden or covered up, they leaked it. They were exceptionally good computer hackers and passionately believed in putting the spotlight on subjects that large corporations and governments preferred to keep quiet. They were heralded by many and despised and feared by the powerful.

John Galt was born in 1949. He was the only son to Mary, an Oxford-educated astrophysicist, and his father Julius. Julius was a Julliard-educated French horn player and composer. His mother was a brilliant physicist and his father was arguably the best French horn player in the world. His parents, the Galts, were smart, educated, and had a sufficiently good sense of humor to name their son John. His name started to became the brunt of jokes when he was about 15 years old. Young John had read all of Rand's works by the time he was 10, so he knew it was just a matter of time until the ribbing began. John was beyond precocious.

When the psychologists tested him, he maxed out on the Miller's Analogy Test while still in his teens, and attained the highest score ever recorded on the Terman Concept Mastery Test. Lewis Terman made it his life's ambition to learn about the intellectually gifted and developed evaluation tools to measure extreme intellectual ability. Lewis Terman had never met anyone like John. The bottom line was that no one could actually measure how smart John was.

John had PhDs in electrical engineering, math, and computer science. He had been a professor, systems designer, security analyst and investment banker. It was in the investment banking community where his name received a lot of the same tired jokes. It usually went something like, "well I guess if John has come back to work this must be a good deal." There were dozens of inane variations on the same theme. John always played along.

Unlike most extraordinarily intelligent people, John could hang. He could disguise his natural abilities and tell Bud-Lite jokes as well as the best of them. After years of easy success in anything, however, he developed an increasing disgust with political leadership. John took his namesake to heart and quietly drifted into nearly complete obscurity. Then, he met Julianne and realized, at long last, that he had found his calling. Finally.

John's computer and hacking skills were among the best. He was a brilliant and creative programmer and could also hack into anything. John had installed dozens of mini-server farms in various locations around the world and had also implemented data delivery systems with dozens of anonymous remailers. Despite the high-speed line he had into his hotel room, it was essentially impossible to trace back to him the messages or data he would drop, for example, in Buenos Aires. For all intents and purposes, John was an invisible man. He managed his efforts on a well-worn-looking Dell computer, the guts of which had been removed and then tricked out in a manner that only a propeller-head of his caliber could pull off. It was as fast as lightning, and had multiple layers of security and encryption. If the machine were accessed incorrectly, violating John's measures to protect against unwanted access, the encryption codes, any memory, and all usage history were designed to literally melt within fifteen seconds.

John's little, common-looking laptop was the world's greatest single-user computer, which he had built for specific purposes.

Comparing it to a car, it was a classic sleeper. It looked a non-descript grey Chevy, but could do zero to sixty in five seconds. If anyone other than John tried to turn it on, the engine would permanently seize with irreparable damage.

John had been bird-dogging several businesses, political causes, and individuals for years. Some because he disliked their nefarious purposes and some because he thought their work was genuinely interesting and had promise. Two of the organizations he watched closely were Bellihurton and HGMP. Two of the many individuals he tracked were Arkloft and Thomas Michael Reynolds. They were at the top of what John called the WWH (the World's Worst Hypocrites) list.

The WWH list was nondenominational and was composed of people who displayed their behavior and thoughts in public or in public policy one way, and behaved the opposite in their personal lives. On his list were people who professed liberal views and promoted inclusive morals in their public lives but went home and beat their wives. He had people like Arkloft and Mike Reynolds who professed moral righteousness and behaved quite differently on their own time. John had hours of videotaped gay sex between these two men, along with drug use and paid sexual partners, both men and women. John was particularly troubled and angered by hypocrisy. He considered it to be a significant contributor to the world's troubles. If people behaved honestly, there would be no need for John to wear two faces. John was acutely aware of the irony of his personal situation, but he could figure no way around it.

John's fundamental belief was not just that the root of all human behavior was fear, and fear's most enduring manifestations were the hate and conflict magnified and promulgated by religion. This cognitive species-level weakness would be the cause of

189

our undoing, this blind conviction that there is only one Kool-aid. Hundreds of religions, each promoting the illogical belief that there is only one true religion—theirs. John considered them all shams and scams. The scriptures were brilliantly written tools of imagination to subjugate the masses, tax the believers, and promote killing in the name of righteousness. Religion had the carrot and stick, the promise of eternal salvation and happiness, and the fear of incomprehensible timeless horror. It was a volatile, vicious combination of psychodynamics for the world's thoughtless, and it was as gratifying and addictive as the Big Mac. Not to say John didn't believe in a higher order. He thought the word God worked well enough. It was short at least. But the idea had really gotten off the leash.

It was in this cynical and contempt-laden context that John found humor and irony, particularly in light of organized religion's current dismissal of basic science; these same disbelievers in science were hiring those in science to fix their problems. Fear of losing the grip trumps faith any time. It builds unholy bonds of symbiotic necessity, and in this case, forged the marriage between HGMP and Bellihurton.

John had been hacking into HGMP for years and was impressed with the scope and quality of their work. The political and ethical compromises were, in John's view, reasonable and acceptable. Everyone couldn't have everything they wanted. When project *Deep Thought* was concocted in the bowels of Bellihurton, John was extremely disgusted at the Cold War tactics that were being exhumed, repurposed, and underwritten by the US government. John had been waiting for the right moment to put Bellihurton in its proper light, and this was the situation he had been waiting for. When HGMP was enlisted as their subcontractor, however, John decided to wait. If HGMP decided to join the Dark Side, he would expose them as well. John also was an acquaintance of Carl Daffin and Julie Perthuis. He had thought they were good human beings. This would be the test to see what side of the fence they were really on.

Since John had hacked into both of the organization's systems, he knew more about Bellihurton's plans for *Deep Thought* than HGMP did. Bellihurton and the Department of Homeland Security had created a vision and plan equal in scope and impact to Mao's plan to cleanse China of its opium-addicted population. *Deep Thought* was tied to a massive jobs program and "social cleansing." It was very similar to ethnic cleansing, but instead of targeting ethnic groups, Deep Thought was going to target "thought groups" or "attitudinal affiliates" as they referred to them.

The jobs plan was that Bellihurton and the DHS were going to build a lot more prisons and would employ thousands of people to build them. Then, they would employ thousands more to staff the prison systems. These employees would watch and retrain the incarcerated. People caught thinking the wrong things, as defined by Homeland Security, would be executed if their thoughts were sufficiently egregious. If the thinking was considered less troublesome, the insurgents would be arrested and sent to re-education camps, all under the aegis of defending real Americans against the threat of global terrorism. And God's word, in the fundamentalist Christian wrappings, would provide the only acceptable food for thought.

There were so many frustrated and angry people in America during this odd post-9/11 period that it was easy to persuade the frustrated and frightened masses to turn against groups of their own as scapegoats. Vilifying the entire Muslim religion and all of its followers had already largely been accomplished. Adding another group or two would be relatively easy. The United States also had considerable experience with large-scale roundups during WWII with the internment camps for the Japanese.

The most infamous and successful implementer of these measures belongs to the one and only Adolf Hitler. Hitler was able to execute his plan largely due to its excellent timing. Hitler's timing was right because Germany's capital markets were out of balance and the economy was in the tank. The population was upset and receptive to radical change. Someone needed to be blamed for tarnishing the Fatherland, and Hitler chose his target carefully. In the case of *Deep Thought*, the time had come. Timing is everything and Homeland believed their timing was now perfect. Their moment had arrived. A new world order was about to be initiated.

John had followed this nefarious project from its inception at Homeland and all the way through the research HGMP had performed. He was aware of their use of psychotropics, and significantly, Julie's "dog ate my homework" security breach.

When the stoners' blogosphere lit-up with tales of great tripping, John suspected it might have had something to do with Julie's security breach, but he wasn't certain. He was certain, however, that the timing was simply too coincidental in light of the research and development HGMP was doing. Although John was about to release a blizzard of damning information on Homeland, Bellihurton, and a few closeted gay boys, he decided to watch and wait for a while. He correctly concluded there was more to come with this story.

With the help of satellite-based geothermal imaging and time-lapse photographic tools, John was able to recreate the early geographic migration of SERPS, its comingling with other fungi, and the subsequent mutations. When he saw the early path from Palo Alto to Jackson Hole, and then a few days later a path from Jackson Hole to Pittsburgh, he checked into Julie's family's credit card and cell phone records. Sure enough, the family had taken a road trip that roughly mirrored the spread of SERPS. The cell phone records led John to their family friends from Pittsburgh. The Percivals' drive home roughly tied-out to the spread of SERPS in the easterly direction.

John hypothesized that Heidi was probably the first canine host. Heidi had eaten the sample from Julie's lab coat and then the sample did what Nature does best—behave in an unpredictable way. Now, there were millions of people tripping all over the world, Twitter and Facebook (now the third largest "Country" on earth) were calling bullshit on the government and espousing the virtues of an expanded consciousness.

John knew about and accepted the virtues associated with mind-expanding drugs. During the 1960s in America, there had been unprecedented social change. The flower children, as they called themselves, were vocal opponents to the Vietnam War and the over-reaching corruption of the Nixon administration. No one knew the exact figure, but hundreds of thousands of people, if not a million, largely college students, dropped acid and took to the streets in protest of an unwinnable war, war profiteering, and the excessive corruption within the military-industrial complex. There was palpable, visible, measurable outrage.

The people's outrage was well-grounded in fact and considered by many to be a good reaction to fundamentally bad thinking, bad values, and bad behavior. The climate and conditions in present-day America were in many ways the same now as they were in the sixties. The country was ten years into a very unpopular war—two, actually. Corruption was rampant. The economy was in trouble. The political leadership was overflowing with acrimony and recriminations and very short on rationality and solutions, but there was no outrage among the people. Why not?

Even though there was very high unemployment, historically high imbalances in compensation and the gap between the rich and poor was the widest in history, there was no outrage. The people seemed resigned or at a minimum, oddly complacent that their money and sense of security had been hijacked by the financial industry and its political puppets.

John's theory was that there was a missing ingredient, a catalyst that had improved awareness in the sixties. Something that had sharpened what he called "the bullshit detector." This missing ingredient, he theorized, was acid. Acid was the ingredient that had opened the eyes and unified the voices of millions of young people. He knew from personal experience, and from a preponderance of persuasive research done by psychiatrists and the military, that acid did, in fact, open the doors of perception. It altered the perception of some part of the electromagnetic wave spectrum. It either filtered out some of the interference or improved the ability to receive other peak wavelength emissions. Or both.

Today, without widespread use of this eye-opening agent, people were more easily lured into complacency. They now waited with great expectations for the next generation iPhone or the next pseudo star; the hyper-popular personalities who offer nothing other than being popular, such as the Karcrashian sisters. Of all the evidence pointing to a society in decline, this phenomenon of hyperattraction to the talentless was the most telling and disturbing for John. The population had been so dumbed-down that they were now transfixed by the comings and goings of people who literally did not merit a second glance. No smart person was left behind.

Chapter Thirty-Three

A s John thought about this circumstance, he concluded he was now part of a seminal moment in man's evolution on Earth. His leaks of political hypocrisy, sexual peccadilloes, and fiscal mismanagement seemed insignificant against the prospect of an enlightened planet. John decided to change his plan. Through the Wikileaks network, John had the capability to deliver a message to around three million people. He decided to trip and tweet, as many others were doing, but with a much larger goal.

It wasn't hard for the man in the street to find SERPS. As John thought about his next move, people were tripping all over the place. Some of these trips were more unusual than others. One such was that of Bruce. Bruce had had eaten some 'shrooms earlier and was now an hour into his trip. Each year, Bruce, a heavyset man with a full white beard, would ride his motorcycle from the Atlantic coast to the Pacific coast, varying his route annually. This year, in late June, he was crossing through southern Canada, and was now in the Province of Saskatchewan. The Canadians joke about the people who live in Saskatchewan, calling them people without hope because the place is just so fucking desolate, with miles and miles of more miles and miles.

Bruce was on a straight road with nothing but cornfields on both sides and now also tripping his ass off. He'd been riding for about six hours and it was now about eleven p.m. His bike's headlight seemed to cut a hole in the darkness, with the white painted lines providing a mesmerizing path. Bruce's mind was unencumbered, flying down the road at a hundred miles an hour. He was both the master of the universe and a speck of dust at the same moment. He was connected to the cosmos. Then, far in the distance he saw light, lots of it, like a cloud. It covered most of the horizon, or at least as far as he could tell. After riding twenty miles, the light became significantly brighter. Twenty-five miles later, Bruce pulled off to the side of the road, turned off his bike and turned off its light.

Now instead of his motorcycle light cutting a path through the darkness, the fields were illuminated. The road and the space above it was like a giant black wall and Bruce was in the middle of it, part of it. On both sides of the road, about twelve inches above the corn stalks, covering dozens of square miles, hovered tens of millions of lightning bugs, each flickering individually but collectively humming with luminescence. It was more magical than a young child's Christmas morning, more gripping and unimaginably wonderful than seeing a child born. Bruce was swaddled in screaming silent harmonies. He had to catch his breath; he fell to the ground and lay on the warm blacktop. He opened his eyes and let go. This show was for him.

While Bruce enjoyed his most life-altering experience, John went down to the bar in the basement of the Union Hotel. It was a wonderful old bar. The exposed-stone walls were two feet thick and been laid by stoneworkers long before the Civil War began. The long bar on the other side of the room could seat twenty.

Behind the bar, the typical collection of liquors and syrupy sweet additives were on display beneath the bright halogen lights. The Pittsburgh Pirates were playing, so there were lots of guys with ball caps and T-shirts sipping Iron City beer and watching the big flat-screen TV monitors. John ordered a beer and made some pleasant comments about the game.

While John was chatting, he looked around the room and saw a couple of guys with mellow grins. After a few minutes, John drifted over to their table to get a closer look. Their pupils were fully dilated and they were in their own world. They were clearly tripping.

John said, "Where are the 'shrooms? I'd like to eat some."

Without a word, one of the guys got up from the table and began walking toward the back door. John followed him outside to his green Ford pickup. The guy reached in the back of the cab and then handed John a small brown paper bag. John reached inside, grabbed one, popped it in his mouth and returned the bag to the guy. John thanked him. No other words were said as the man walked back to the bar.

Within thirty seconds, John was beginning to feel the effects. Within five minutes, he was tripping much more profoundly than he had ever tripped before, and he'd dropped acid that had come directly from the Sandoz Laboratories. The Sandoz acid was otherworldly and cosmic, but this stuff catapulted him into a much different distortion of time and space. He sensed the presence of others having the same reaction. When John walked back through the bar, he gave his new friends a thankful smile and noticed there was faint aura around each of them. They actually had a glow. They were emitting something. The same glow came from a few others sitting in the bar. They gave John a quick and approving "welcome to the club" sort of look. John had never seen anything quite like this. John could clearly differentiate two types of people in the bar, those emitting a visible vibe and those who weren't. John's first question was whether or not the perception was pre-retinal. Was he simply picking this up or was he seeing this with his eyes? John knew that some psychedelic imagery was non-retinal in nature. At this moment, he didn't particularly care, but he wanted to remember the idea for later, when he could follow a thought for longer than a nanosecond.

John had no intention of staying indoors. This was a beautiful warm day and he had a beautiful consciousness going on that was getting progressively more intense.

He headed outside and walked to the river's edge where he lay in the grass and let his big brain drift through undulating waves of endless thought in the multidimensional confluence of time and space. Pools of sorrow and waves of joy were drifting through his open mind as if they were possessing and caressing him. He felt limitless undying love shining around him like a million suns. Words were flying out like endless rain into a paper cup and images of broken light danced before him like a million eyes. They slithered while they passed and slipped away across the universe. His thoughts meandered like a restless wind inside a letterbox and they tumbled blindly as they made their way across the universe.[6]

It was an experience that transcended time, space, life, and description. Words were without purpose. He seemed to be living a full lifetime, or more. The immediacy of the moment eclipsed everything. There was no past, there was no future. It was only the here and now. This went on for an unmeasured period of time. Then, as if a light switch had been clicked off, it was over. John was back to normal consciousness, but with the indelible memory and awareness that he had just been changed forever and for the better. John was now a new citizen of something much bigger than the world. John now knew that he would help change the world. John went to the upstairs bar in the Union, and sat in the antique barber's chair with a double bourbon in hand. John didn't drink much or often, but this moment required a cocktail.

Chapter Thirty-Four

John finished his drink and then returned to his room and took a short nap. He had learned decades ago that napping pays big dividends. It pays to sleep on important things. The mind has a remarkable capacity to sort things out while sleeping and set good foundations for taking action. Even with John's encyclopedic knowledge of so many subjects, he did not connect sleep with Schumann's Resonance.

After John took a shower and refreshed himself, his plan had crystallized. He would use his network to help organize a coordinated, global event. The event would coincide with the next full moon, which would present itself in two days. The full moon was an event the whole world could recognize. The object was to have as many people as possible within a twenty-four-hour period share in the same extra-psychotropic experience. His first communication to around 800,000 people was, "Tried the 'shrooms, fantastic beyond words, stay tuned."

Within an hour, the web lit up as if it had been given a shot of adrenalin. Only a few people within the Wikileaks organization could freely use the entire contacts database, but John could do more or less as he pleased. Now, with a multiplier effect, an estimated billion people were officially tuned in to this unfolding global phenomenon. The 'shrooms were now, literally, everywhere on earth. Even in countries where digital communication was censored, the word was spreading, if not digitally, then the old-fashioned way, word of mouth. From Lhasa to Lima, from Johannesburg to Janesville, Wisconsin, people were riveted to this phenomenon. More and more people were eating the 'shrooms and more and more people believed much less in what they saw on TV and heard on the radio. News journalism was, for the time being, officially dead. If you wanted to figure out what was going on, hit the web, follow tweets and stay glued to your Facebook page. The governments had completely lost the reins in message management and media control. They contemplated shutting down the web, but quickly realized too many of their own systems were dependent upon it. All bets were off. It was truly a brave new world.

John watched and read as much as he could. The well-constructed social systems and communication methods were unraveling, and with remarkably little chaos. It was a sight to behold. It was marvelous in the truest sense of the word. There was civil disobedience, but it was for the most part simply widespread apathy and passive antipathy toward authority. People disobeyed, but in a civilized way. En masse, millions blew off authority figures and walked away. No riots. No broken windows. No smoke bombs trying to control roving mobs with stolen TV sets. No, this was a massive display of, "I'm aware as Hell and I'm not going to take it anymore."

The TV networks, Hound News leading the way, showed "live" news feeds of riots, people vomiting and convulsing due to the adverse reactions of eating toxic mushrooms. The phenomenon was quickly classified as biological terrorism and a branch of al Qaeda was listed as the main villain. The problem was though, that a rapidly increasing number of people, young and old, red and yellow, black and tan, conservative and liberal, just were not buying it. Their bullshit detectors were now working perfectly.

The next day John sent out his next message, "Let's all eat together. Tell everyone. Get prepared. Details to follow." It was like the web got another shot in the arm. John estimated that roughly a third of the world's population was doing nothing other than staying tuned. Business stopped or significantly slowed everywhere. The roads were not clogged with traffic. People were staying close to their homes, family, and friends. It was a bad time to order a pizza, because no one was delivering.

Chapter Thirty-Five

J ohn's next and final message read, "Eat and watch the full moon @ 8 p.m. GMT." At 8 p.m. GMT, an estimated two billion people ate SERPS together under the presence of the bright round moon. Two billion people had their brains simultaneously humming at 7.83 Hz. Two billion people were in electromagnetic harmony with the light of the moon, under the umbrella of Schumann's Resonance. From the space station, the astronauts could see the earth's landmasses changing color. They communicated to mission control that photo-phosphorescent tendrils of a turquoise-like blue were spreading and becoming brighter by the minute. It was astounding to see. The planet was glowing and pulsing.

Then two astonishing events took place.

The first event involved the combined energy of the two billion simultaneously actively tripping humans. These folks had eaten their 'shrooms and were tripping like no one had ever tripped before. It was a magical transcendental moment because they felt one another. They felt a bond, a kinship, a shared understanding. Then, the absolutely unimaginable occurred. Their consciousness jumped.

It jumped to every other person on earth, regardless of location, use of masks, or special secure facilities; it didn't matter. Even the astronauts were affected. Everyone was literally now on the same wavelength, and specifically, 7.83 Hz. All of humankind was buzzing with the full moon. John's message was the catalyst that created a tipping point. This wasn't part of John's plan, but it was obviously part of someone's or something's plan.

Something else happened. Everything that was moving stopped moving—in place. Everything. Airplanes that were a foot above the landing strip stopped in mid-air. Elevators and escalators stopped wherever they were. Baseballs in their flights stopped. Rivers stopped. Rain stopped. All cars, trains, busses, bikes; they were all frozen in their spots. Watches and clocks stopped. Everything was as still as a photo. Everyone was aware of it and no one did anything except pay attention. People could move, but there was no interest in even thinking about it. Everyone from prince to pauper to prisoner to pioneer had their minds fixed on only one thing, the message in their heads. They were listening to a voice that was inaudible.

Everyone received the same message. It wasn't so much that they *heard* the message, but rather, absorbed it. The message was delivered to people in their own languages with their own accents and their own idioms. Although it appeared to "sound" like the spoken word, the world was completely devoid of sound. Nothing was moving.

The message was...

> *Congratulations, humans of Earth. You have reached a crowning moment in your progress as a species. You have achieved enlightenment. You have avoided what we thought was your predictable fate, self-annihilation by*

greed, aggression, and abuse of technology. This has been the fate of your two predecessor civilizations on Earth.

The two civilizations on Earth before your current one each died and along with them, most other life forms on your planet. That's why you occasionally find something you can't reconcile with history as you know it. Each of your predecessor civilizations had advanced to an evolutionary stage close to the one you are currently experiencing. Unfortunately, they each created global war and, with weapons of mass destruction, contaminated the earth to a point where all livings things died. One civilization did this with biological technology and the other with nuclear or radioactive technology. In each case, the human population and most of the other supporting life forms were wiped out. It took hundreds of millions of years before humans re-evolved to the stage where they would pursue technology. Technology is but one of the available evolutionary paths toward singularity.

Our species has existed for trillions of years and we have watched your planet with great interest, as we do with many others. There are millions of inhabited stones just like yours throughout the vast expanse that you refer to as the universe. Our purpose is to perpetuate life and life-energy. Our goal is to create systems that sustain life energy. These systems have a central energy source for light and heat, among other things. Many of the stones also have smaller orbiting stones that assist in energy management.

You are new and young to technology and have only a superficial understanding of some of the basic elements of physics, even gravity, for example. You are close to understanding gravity, but have overlooked a few useful tools. Some of your recent predecessor civilizations understood these fundamentals and this understanding allowed them

*to build and create physical structures far more advanced
than with the other technologies they had at their disposal.*

As the message continued, it became clear that the communicator had a sense of humor. It seemed to have a personality also, one that was like a combination of Mel Brooks, Henny Youngman and the Dalai Lama, for those hearing it in America anyway. It had dry wit coupled with the wisdom of the ages.

*We have observed similar life forms develop many times.
Some of the stones, such as your earth, survive and prosper
and others, many of them, die for a number of reasons.
Overpopulation, the disregard and misuse of natural resources, and excessive greed and aggression are the most
common reasons for catastrophic and terminal failure. We
have found only one ingredient that helps overcome these
terminal pitfalls, and we leave it up to the life forms to
discover it for themselves. It's sort of a pass-fail test. The
stones that discover it and use it live long and prosper.
Those that don't, generally self-destruct. Along with paths
to enlightenment, we have built competing forces. These
are the forces of darkness and aggression; the forces of so
called evil and the bad. These competing forces produce energy, self-reflection, the need for societal management, the
need for governance and the quest for the* raison d'être.
*These forces do not go away now, even though you have
passed a significant milestone. On the contrary, you must
now not only be aware of this reality, but embrace its existence and remain* en garde *against its extreme risks. With
the new tools you will have at your disposal, there will be
extreme temptation to abuse knowledge and power, with
forces that you cannot even imagine. So, check yourselves.*

While we have your undivided attention, let's get a few things straight. For starters, evolution is real. We started you guys off with a bit of germ seed so to speak. It's kind of like yeast; gets things going. From there, one little life form morphs and changes and pretty soon, there you are: intelligent, self-aware, sentient beings—you, the humans. With sentience came questions of life's origin, life's meaning and the need for a higher, omnipotent being.

But you have the god thing all wrong. Yes, there is a higher power. I'm it. I, we, whatever, get the ball rolling, and after that it is up to you. Every single thing on earth is there for a reason, it is up to you to figure out why and put your resources to good and proper use, develop productive and useful moral and ethical compasses and advance yourselves with out killing the goose that lays the golden eggs – the planet itself.

And while we're on the subject of higher powers, what's up with all of these religions? They speak to your slow progress toward understanding the meaning of life; but I'll get back to that in a minute. Each of your religions is equally right and equally wrong. For starters, there can't be just one correct religion and the rest wrong. Since each of a given religion's followers believes their religion is the only correct one, logically you all have to be wrong. Hey, these religions are all basically the same story with a different fictional lead man to look up to and admire. On that subject, where are the important girl gods?

But let me get back to my main point, you have Mohammad, Jesus, Buddha, and all of those Hindu gods, Brahma and all of those lesser gods of Krishna, Vishnu, Kali, Saraswati, Rama, Lakshmi. I get tired just going through the list. Then if that's not enough, you've created seemingly endless subcategories that simply confuse people and create unavoidable opportunities for friction. The Catholics, the Protestants, the Jews, the Reformed Jews, the Orthodox Jews, the Conservative Jews, the Lutherans, the Baptists, enough already.

I want to stick to my promise and get back to the meaning of life. It is really pretty simple. Everything in the universe is just the way it's supposed to be. Period. Enjoy it and help others do the same. That's it. It's real simple. The more of the good you do, the more of the good you get. This insight was paraphrased by one of your artists several years ago when he wrote that "in the end, the love you take is equal to the love you make." *he actually ripped off the thought from William Shakespeare, which is fine by us. It's sort of the nature of evolution as we have engineered it; everything is built on something before itself. That is to say, all things—living or conceptual—are derivative. One begets the next.*

While I'm on the subject of good, what's with all the 25,000 square foot houses? These places are big enough for entire tribes. The idea is to share in the bounty of the stone as you progress toward singularity. Sure, some people can earn more than others, hoard more than others; that's okay and we encourage some of it. But enough already with excessive excess. That big stretch of beach shouldn't belong to just one fat guy. Now that I've opened the door on fat, you guys in the so-called developed countries, enough with the gratuitous fat. I like a little butter or olive oil as much as the next guy, but people, hear me out on this one, lighten up on the fries and oversized burgers. Eat more vegetables, particularly mushrooms. Very low in calories.

I could go on for weeks, but am going to sign off in a minute. Before I do, I want to manage your expectations a bit.

First, time has been stopped. When I turn it back on again, everything will resume as it was before I put all of you on hold. Two, you will each remember this, and vividly. So, recognize and accept your place in the vastness of our universe. You as individuals and the stone that you call your earth are small participating elements in an unimaginably large expanse of time and space. You will develop a greater understanding for this as you continue to evolve, but today you have made the most important step in your progress. You have found the foodstuff that opens the great door, as I like to call it. Once you get the speed of light under control, lots of cool stuff happens. By the way, it's not the fastest speed. It's up there, but there's faster travel. Thought, for example, is really fast. I'll explain a lot more stuff in a few minutes. You see, I get distracted easily.

Be honest. Be good. Be helpful. Be respectful of all things, be they human, lower species, plants or minerals. Oh, I almost forgot, dial back the population if you elect to stay Earthbound. Your stone works really well with around 2.5 billion people. You have a lot of work to do. And remember evil still lurks in the most unlikely places. Stay on your toes.

The voice continued for a full cycle of the moon, 28 days to the second. It explained all kinds of science and medicine. It answered all of the heretofore unanswerable questions. It provided the path to traveling at light speed, it explained how to use the Bose-Einstein condensate, it explained how to miniaturize nuclear power and safely reuse its waste, it explained the physics and astronomy behind Leedskalnin's achievements, it explained Atlantis, Egypt, and Machu Picchu.

Then the voice said, "Good-bye and good luck."

Chapter Thirty-Six

S uddenly, everything began to move again. The plane that was a foot above the field touched down as planned. Traffic lights resumed their normal operations; the second baseman caught the batter's hit and the hum of everyday life resumed. Within minutes though, people who were driving found a place to park. They got out of their cars and had a conversation with a stranger. Their trips were over, but everyone had participated in precisely the same experience. Their lives were changed forever.

A few days later on the evening comedy news shows had a different perspective.

Jon Stewart opened by turning into the camera with that famous sarcastic, deadpan grin and said, "I don't know about you, but I think he sounded a lot like Mel Brooks." And with that, he introduced his guest for the evening, Bull O'Really. Bull had a show on the Hound News channel, referred to by people who did not share his views as, "The No Grin Zone." Their differences were now behind them.

O'Really started talking and said, "You know, I never thought you were actually a bad guy, we just were on different sides of the entertainment business. You have your audience and I had mine. We fed each other's successes. You know my employers, they wanted to control everything. I was asked to attend the Board meeting after Mel or whatever his name is gave us our lecture. They have changed the focus of their ambitions. They now see that the type of control they were seeking is pointless. They have however, been given the most remarkable set of scientific and medical tools imaginable and they want to manage them as best as possible for the people. Somebody's got to manage it, so why not us?"

Stephen Colbert flipped his head around and announced with excitement, "Nation, there is now confirmation of life beyond Texas, and it's all over the place."

Bill Maher opened his monologue by saying, "Well, we've all heard the news. It's kind of a good-news–bad-news story, particularly for me. The good news is that the religious wars are over. You know how I feel about religion. The bad news is, my career as a political critic is over. Moshe or Mohamed or Jesus or whatever the fuck his name is, you notice he didn't even tell us his name— What's up with that? Where are your manners? Anyway, he answered all the big questions. I don't have anything to bitch about anymore. I can't tell you how happy that makes me. But, Moshe did tip his hand a bit. There's evil still lurking. Maybe I'm just an incurable cynic, but we could still fuck things up and I could be recalled to perform my duty to be the flag waver of critical thinking. I hope I'm wrong, but you never know."

Howard Stern turned to his sidekick Robin and said, "We don't even have to fuck now. I'm over it. I feel great. I've fired my therapist. I'm a new man."

Radio and TV journalists all over the world made similar comments. It was a new ballgame.

Chapter Thirty-Seven

Rob resumed his dog-walking job, and played a lot more music. One day, as he was returning Heidi to her home, Julie was in the yard pulling some weeds. As Rob walked toward Julie he thought to himself, I'd really like to bang her, she is one hot MILF. He knew it wasn't cool, however, and that it wasn't going to happen.

When he got close to Julie, she stood up.

"Hello Dr. Perthuis," he said.

Then he looked her straight in the eyes for about seven seconds and neither said a word. Rob knew then that she knew that Rob knew how the whole thing started.

Rob said, "Dr. Perthuis, I was probably the first person to eat them, in their early stage before they morphed and dispersed. Thank you."

Julie said, "No, thank you, too. I knew someone had to help stir the pot, and now it all makes sense."

Epilogue

This had been the meme of all memes, the *Ubermeme*. There had been a symbiotic tsunami blending human consciousness with a sympathetic catalyst inherent in certain fungi that rewired the human brain. With this shared experience, there had been a complete reorientation of the human race. Life on Earth would never be the same. The battle between Hegel and Buddha was over. The battle between Yoda and Vader had been concluded, or so everyone thought anyway. Good had won again, but this time, it seemed to have a truly enduring quality. The nature of life, its inherent struggles and its reason for being had been answered, simply, profoundly and with the knowledge to advance societies of all types and humankind in general. The profound recalibration of thought, the merits of ambition, and the tools for change also came with an ominous warning – there were still threats, now presumably better camouflaged than in the past.

Over the next decade, the world's activities and those of industry, science, education, and medicine shifted dramatically. Where there was once contention there was now consensus. Where there was once division, there was now direction. The people of Earth now had a better understanding of their purpose and understood new tools to help in their advance of it. Things were returned to an earlier, natural balance. The human brain was now used to its potential and people did much more of what Aristotle had described as good things. The people on the third stone from the sun were now *experienced.*

The humans' next big leap came about fifty years later. Some humans concluded that their biological life support systems were inherently inefficient. They decided, in large numbers, to abandon them and leave their bodies behind. In an instant hundreds of millions of people left their bodies behind and opted for a life of consciousness, free from the toils of basic survival and competition. Many others elected to remain on a more verdant and balanced planet. It was now intelligently managed and there were few issues. The discarded bodies were buried in thousands of mass pits and the mycelium did their jobs of consuming the remains. The excess rubbish left behind, the manmade relics of metal, plastic, glass, and other materials, were repurposed or disintegrated. Much of earth was returned to a wilderness state, with vast expanses of land left to the forces of nature. Oil was a relic of the past and took its position next to the steam engine as an example of human's historic quest for energy. Most of the world's most effective and viral-like and inhabitant-predator, man, had been taken out of the biologic and environmental mix. With the energy of the humans' thoughts coupled with the energy of the earth's output, their species lived on in relative peace.

A large part of the human race now resided with the collective consciousness, memories, emotions, and aspirations of all who had lived before them. It was all in the cloud. Once in the cloud, each individual became part of a shared body of information and in the sense of quantum physics, all things became one and one became all things. Singularity had been achieved. Collective singularity.

As for the main actors in this advance of humankind, Julie, Clark, and family opted for the cloud, as did Earp. Sally and Rob stayed behind. Rob took his ill-gotten gains from 'shroom selling and produced his own music. He also returned to school to study organic chemistry and psychomycology. His music became extraordinarily popular and he achieved fame that made the Karcrashians—a pointless family that had dropped back into well-deserved obscurity within days of the singularity—look like shut-ins. In many ways this was good because he could promote his messages and opinions. But the fame and adulation brought along with it exposure to risks and temptations that he was not prepared to handle. Julie had introduced Rob to Paulo before she made the jump, figuring they would find common ground. There were no drugs or spiritual leaders in the universe strong enough to fully diminish Paulo's narcissistic competitive drive and his insatiable quest to achieve.

One evening, much to Sally's great dismay, she received a late night call from Rob. He explained that he was with Paulo and apologized for falling off the wagon. He rambled for a bit about building upon what had been started. How things and life could be even better. He told her he'd had a vision.

Sally said, "Good night."

Afterword

The Origin of Life on Earth

One of the first credible, modern thinkers and scientists to delve into life's origin on earth was Francis Harry Compton Crick. Crick was a biophysicist. He was credited, along with his partner James D. Watson, with discovering the structure of deoxyribonucleic acid or DNA. DNA is often referred to as "the keeper of the code." With a complete record of a life form's attributes and composition, each piece of DNA is, so to speak, a full system. Everything needed to recreate a living thing or part of a living thing is stored in this tiny piece of code. Considering the difficulties each of us has simply backing up our personal hard drives or keeping track of varying versions of a project's content, or even phone numbers, having a complete set of compatible, functional variables or attributes that make up a living thing in its totality, all packed into a little microscopic package, is truly remarkable.

Imagine the thrill these two young researchers must have felt when they realized what they had discovered. Consider also that for a brief period of time, they were the only two people alive who knew this stunning discovery and its significance. The well-deserved congratulatory beers in the pub that night for these two doctoral students didn't just punctuate the culmination of a complex piece of research, but also set the wheels in motion for work that would change the world in many ways. Their discovery was the biological equivalent of discovering Pi or specific gravity. Fueled by tireless curiosity, the next questions Crick and Watson couldn't avoid if they had wanted to try were *the why*s and *how*s.

The 1950s and 1960s, were home to various ideas about how life began. Some of these ideas were based on research; some based on religious faith, and others on speculative fiction. Many of these early ideas still influence the way we think about the origins of life today. Consider the current proposed curriculum changes in the Oklahoma public education system. Surrounding these proposed changes is the passionate debate regarding the validity of the Theory of Evolution. Was the Garden of Gethsemane part of a process, the end of a process, the result of a download from God, or just an easy visualization of a psychologically calming allegory?

A crucial experiment, which apparently demonstrated how life might have started through purely natural means, was published in May of 1953. This was shortly after Watson and Crick published their groundbreaking paper on DNA. The Nobel Prize winning chemist Harold Urey was working on the separation of uranium for use in the atom bomb. After the Second World War, Urey switched his interests from practical physics, to the origins of the planets and the origin of life on Earth and elsewhere. Urey became interested in prior notions about the chemical origins of life that had been proposed about 30 years earlier. In the 1920s,

Russian scientist A.I. Oparin and British biologist J.B.S. Haldane proposed a means by which life could have started through a simple chemical reaction—without the intervention of a creator. They suggested that life could have been started by combining a specific mix of chemicals in the Earth's early atmosphere with an accidental spark.

It was this work that Urey and his student Miller glommed onto. Stanley Miller, one of Urey's pupils, offered to conduct experiments to demonstrate that, with the right mixture of chemicals coupled with just the right electrical charge, under just the right conditions, life could have been started. The analytical tool was chromatography. The test trials were constructed to look for variations and changes in peak wave length emissions, with the understanding that each element has its own peak wavelength.

At the end of one week, Miller observed that as much as 10–15 percent of the carbon was now in the form of organic compounds. Two percent of the carbon had formed some of the amino acids that are used to make proteins. Perhaps most important, Miller's experiment showed that organic compounds such as amino acids, which are essential to cellular life, could be "made easily" under the conditions that scientists believed to be present on neonatal Earth.

This monumental finding inspired a multitude of further experiments. The implication (their conclusion) was that these perfect conditions had in fact been present at a specific point in the earth's past. It was at this point in prehistoric time that the now famous "primeval or primordial soup" was created and life began. It was this unique chemical porridge that produced the microorganisms that became the foundation and essential building blocks of life as we now know it.

Miller and Urey made particular assumptions about Earth's

early atmosphere that are no longer shared by contemporary scientists, nor is their emphasis on the protein origin of early life. Their work, however, stimulated many others to pursue similar paths. The discussion about the chemical origin of life and the homey, memorable metaphor of primordial soup remain a strong foundation for the "natural start" argument.

The theory that life began with a chance reaction of chemicals was particularly popular with the Russian Communist Party in the fifties and sixties. For them, the material basis of everything was of political as well as scientific importance. For them, life could be seen to resemble a highly complex modern machine, an extension of the complex political machine the Communists aggressively promoted. Describing the origins of life in this manner enabled the Communist Party to present a vision of the universe without a God. Haldane and Oparin, and Miller and Urey, created a convenient set of constructs and theories to support a strong and emerging political ideology and, its associated military complex. Basic chemistry had created life. That is, an industrial process.

This mix of theories mentioned above is *Theory One*.

The next, and oldest, theory is the religious theory. It was and still is a very simple theory: God did it.

This is *Theory Two*.

As convenient as these two theories were in furthering political or religious agendas, they left the door open for other questions and precious few answers. Principal among them was the idea that the origin of life on Earth had Extra-terrestrial roots.

This is *Theory Three*.

In the 1950s, *The Eagle* comic was launched with its hero, Dan Dare. This was just part of the modern, popular culture that was increasingly focused on extra-terrestrial life. Speculation about what might exist amongst and beyond the stars was not new thought, but with advances in technology, the advent of computer-assisted problem solving and the emerging field of commercial aviation, the explicitly vague and unintelligible nature of the universe became a breeding ground for science fiction, speculative philosophy, and, serious research. In the 1990s, the generously funded Search for Extra-Terrestrial Intelligence (SETI) project was launched. Its purpose was to search for intelligent life elsewhere in the universe and link this search with theories about the origins of life on Earth.

Francis Crick became very interested in this idea that life on Earth came from outer space. With Crick taking a seat on the dais, there was now a person of stature embracing an idea that otherwise would have had great difficulty taking roots and getting serious attention. If the man that who discovered DNA thought any idea had merit, it did. Crick got deeply into the subject and wrote a book entitled *Life Itself: Its Origins and Nature*. In it he takes a provocative position: that the seeds of life were thrown into the black vastness of space and found a hospitable environment on earth. Once here, they took root, evolved, and mutated, and here we are. In the book's introduction, Crick writes, "I explore a variant of Panspermia. To avoid damage, the microorganisms are supposed to have traveled in the head of an unmanned spaceship sent to earth by a higher civilization, which had developed somewhere billions of years ago. The spaceship was unmanned so its range would be as great as possible. Life started here when these organisms were dropped into the primitive ocean and began to multiply."

With Crick's tremendous stature in the fields of chemistry and biophysics, others promoted related theories supporting the notion that life on earth somehow *landed* here, rather than being an organic, freak accident of nature. Not coincidentally, Urey became another supporter. Urey had had a good whiff of the primordial soup's bouquet, but it left him hungry for the whys and wherefores. Later in Urey's life, he helped develop the field of "cosmochemistry" and is credited with coining the term. His work on oxygen-18 led him to develop theories about the abundance of various chemical elements on Earth and of their abundance and evolution in the stars. Urey's work was pioneering in this highly esoteric area of paleoclimatic research. Urey summarized his theories and work in *The Planets: Their Origin and Development.* Urey speculated that the early terrestrial atmosphere was composed of ammonia, methane, and hydrogen. With the help of Stanley L. Miller, his University of Chicago graduate students, he knew that a well-timed mixture of chemicals, exposed to electric sparks and water, could create a chemical reaction and produce amino acids, the essential foundation for life. This theory, for all of its technical merit, seemed shallow and begged far too big questions. So these luminaries in their fields looked up into the vastness of space for better answers.

The Tenets of Technology

Although the idea of a giant spaceship chocked full of high-tech gadgetry hurling itself through space has visual and romantic appeal, it seems an unlikely scenario due to the two primary and well-established tenets of technology. History has given us innumerable examples and taught us these two important lessons, and done so largely over the past seven hundred years or so. Not much time when you think about the age of Earth and life's documented history on the planet.

The first tenet is that as technology improves, it becomes progressively smaller and migrates closer and closer to the end user. Big Ben was the first clock. One had to walk near enough to Ben to read it. Now the timepiece is but a string of code housed in most cell phones.

The first places for entertainment centers were open-air theaters with one performance and one crowd. Theater morphed into film and soon there were movie theaters. The theater soon became the "home theater" mounted on the wall or in a special room. Now it's in your smartphone.

Cameras were once the tools of the wealthy and were large, complex, and cumbersome. If cinematography was required, so was the expertise of someone with the equipment and expertise. Now, tiny cameras can be ingested giving physicians and researchers an up-close-and-personal view of last night's dinner as it winds its way through the intestinal tract.

The second major tenet is that as the technology improves, specifically information technology, it becomes progressively more powerful, and equally important, does so at an increasingly faster rate. Technology, by its nature begets better and faster technology. This tenet is now referred to as a Law—Moore's Law. This law states that every eighteen months or so microprocessors become twice as powerful as their predecessor's. It is interesting to look backward to see the impact this law has had on computing. It is nothing short of breathtaking to roll the math forward for a hundred or two hundred years—a thousand years—and fantasize about what life will be like with these advances. We should be free of biological needs at some point.

Logic, therefore, would dictates that if Earth was visited by extra-terrestrial life, that life arrived here in a very small, if not invisible, package. The package would not only be small, but exceptionally powerful, complex, and efficient. It would be an offensive and defensive tour de force. It would be able to reproduce, create its own food sources, and more or less survive and prosper on its own volition. Coupling aspects of each of these theories, the likelihood that there was a helping hand in getting the ball of life rolling on Earth has significant intuitive appeal. Crick's early theories on the mechanics of panspermia seem inconsistent with what we've learned about the tenets of technology. The notion of panspermia, however, seems to have significantly more merit today than it might have when it was introduced.

The Fungi, Earth's Most Important, Enduring, and Populous Life Form

There is no such thing as flour without mold. This is an astonishing fact known by almost no one. Fungi, which include large mushrooms, cultures that are tiny, cultures that cover square miles, molds we can see and not smell, molds we can smell and not see, and to the microflora that can be seen only with the aid of microscopes are the most populous, creative, and ubiquitous life form on earth. Fungi are literally all around us all of the time. We eat, breathe, or drink some form of a fungus every day. Usually this is only in the form of consuming their seeds or spores. But not a day goes by without some type of intimate encounter with a fungus. Don't believe it? Take a little dust from under the sofa cushions or the dust under the rug, add it to a little bit of potato liquid or agar, some salt and sugar in the right combination, and in a few days mushrooms or fungi will start to show themselves. The mushrooms, or more precisely their "fruits," are the things we see. We see them in forests, fields, and grocery stores. We see them in our yards, in parks, growing on trees, growing on oranges left in the basket too long, or bread left too long in the drawer. They are literally everywhere. These things we see and eat with great alacrity are essentially the reproductive structures of fungi. These rubber-like things we see are there solely for the purpose of throwing off spores. Or at least as far as we've been able to figure out so far. These fruits are what most people associate with mushrooms.

Our superficial level of awareness of fungi is nothing short of frightening, considering their significance to human's existence, the earth's biological stability, and the maintenance of our ecosystems. They are the most important living things on earth. There would be no life on Earth without fungi. The planet and its living inhabitants would choke, drown, and suffocate on their own waste. Flesh and vegetation would not rot. Things would not biodegrade. Dead animal and vegetable flesh would pile up rapidly. Fungi are our best friends and hardest workers, being both our garbage men and the fertilizers of our gardens.

Mushrooms have two basic stages to their life cycle. They have a vegetative stage where their mycelium or the supporting life system forms. The mycelium is essentially a root system. The mycelium collects water and the nutrients needed for growth. The second stage is a reproductive stage and is dedicated to spore reproduction. Mushrooms reproduce by mitosis; that is, their cells divide and produce identical offspring. No mating is needed. Once a fertile host is established, mushrooms quickly germinate and form a network of tiny thread-like cells. This mycelium performs the asexual reproductive chores to perpetuate the mushroom. As part of their life cycle, a mature mushroom discharges millions of microscopic spores from its gills or pores. Six thousand mushrooms produce more spores than there are people on earth. These parts of their anatomy, the gills, are typically found under the cap.

The fungus family is incomprehensibly vast in its diversity. We are generally familiar with only the edibles—the fat portobello we grill, the tasty porcini in our risotto, the sautéed white buttons garnishing our filet or the exotic truffle that is good with anything. These are the fungi we know and love. As tasty as they are, they tell no stories. A walk on the wild side to the boundaries of plant pathology and mycology is needed to get a glimpse of what sustains us. It is truly a very, very bizarre life.

Consider one of the more interesting and nearly universal players, the nematode predator and its fungal partner. Although the vast majority of fungi are obligate saprophytes being biologically forced to subsisting on only things dead, these clever fungal predators prey on the living. Nematodes are worms, sometimes referred to as eel worms because they resemble eels. They are typically less than a millimeter in length. "Most soil is literally filled with nematodes. Some of them invade the roots of plants and some cause diseases. The nematodes, which live a free and independent life in the soil, encounter various hazards. One of these is certain fungi that have found these little animals to be choice food, so much so that certain molds subsist almost entirely on a diet of living nematodes. This requires some ingenuity on the part of the fungus, because nematodes, while small by our standards, are hundreds of times the size of the molds that trap them. Also they are strong, slippery, elusive, and constantly moving—seemingly difficult game for a stationary and delicate fungus to trap and invade. Certain molds, however, have devised some ingenious ways of catching these worms on the squirm, and have become surprisingly adept at this big-game hunting.

The fungus grows through the soil with ordinary branched mycelium, like the mycelium of a thousand other fungi. At frequent intervals short branches grow out from this mycelium and these join to make minute loops or snares. There are likely to be thousands of nematodes and yards of mycelium of this predatory mold in any teaspoon of ordinary black soil in your garden or even in the flowerpot on the windowsill. In his restless, sightless search for food, the nematode will occasionally, by ill chance for him and good chance for the mold, stick his slender, tapering head through one of these many small loops on the mycelium. Contact with his body causes this living snare to contract quickly but briefly; the delicate mycelium, however, is flexible enough to yield with his threshing, and the strangle hold seldom is broken.

It should be obvious that these nematode-hunting fungi are specialists of a rather advanced sort. Certainly millions of years must have been required for their evolution. Delicate and clever adaptations such as they have do not arise suddenly and out of the blue. Man was fairly well along on the road to evolution before he had the wit to make snares, and no man-made can equal those designed by the nematode-snaring fungi."[1] Let's look at another predacious killer molds, *Endothia parisitica*. Endothia parisitica causes chestnut blight. "It was introduced into the United States around 1900, and in the next forty years eliminated almost 100 per cent of the commercially valuable stands of chestnut in the country. Its phenomenal success is due partly to the number of spores it produces and to the variety of ways in which these spores are spread. The mycelium of Endothia invades the bark of the chestnut trees through small wounds, such as those made by the claws of squirrels or woodpeckers, grows through, kills and digests the bark, and within a couple of weeks begins to produce tiny, pimple-like fruit bodies just beneath the surface of the bark. These begin as solid clumps of mycelium. Each clump or knot of mycelium grows until it ruptures the outer layers of bark and so is exposed to the air. As this clump of mycelium, destined to

---

1   Christensen, C.M. (1951). *The Molds and Man*, Oxford University Press, pp. 153–156

become a fruit body, enlarges, a cavity is formed within it, and a narrow channel is formed to connect this chamber with the exposed surface. Stalks grow out from the walls of this cavity, a spore is formed on the tip of each stalk, released as soon at it is mature, another is formed, and so on, until the cavity is filled with millions of spores, all of them embedded in a sticky matrix. This matrix has the ability to absorb water and swell rapidly. When moistened by rain, it swells; spores and matrix are forced out of the fruit body in the form of a yellow tendril. A single one of these small, pimple-like fruit bodies, technically known as a pycinidium, may exude half a billion to a billion spores. It is not uncommon for at least fifty of these fruit bodies to be produced per square inch of bark. On a heavily infected tree there are literally dozens of square feet densely populated with such fruit bodies. The number of spores produced is incalculable."[2]

"In the tropics some of the termites make tremendous nests, in portions of which they cultivate mushrooms or other fungi for food. Unlike the leaf-cutting ants, they do not depend for food solely on the fungus, but often they cultivate it in much the same manner, though on not so large a scale, in special chambers within the nest. That is, certain rooms within their nests will be devoted to the growing of fungi, and a special caste of workers will care for these gardens. One kind of termite builds aboveground nests of adobe clay that are shaped almost exactly like a giant mushroom—a rather remarkable case of nature imitating nature. Usually the fungus is fed to the young of all castes, but after the young have reached a certain stage they get no more of this invigorating food. The royalty, or reproductive castes, are fed it continuously. Not only is it the privilege of the termite upper crust to eat wantonly of mushrooms, but it is this diet that in

---

2   Ibid., pp. 27–28

part makes them socially elite. It recently has been found that a fungus cultivated by one kind of termite contains special growth-promoting vitamins. Obviously these fungi on which ants and termites subsist should be investigated more thoroughly: what is of such great use to them may be of some use to us, not only in the way of commercial gain, but also in advancing the good life."[3]

Another interesting example of insects relishing the food produced by fungi is the ambrosia beetle. They have created structures on their heads in the form of miniature baskets. It is in these baskets that they carry the spores of their special fungus—that ambrosia used for food—from their old home to their new one. And some wonder about evolution....

Rusts. First, most people have never even heard of them. "The rust fungi are not very numerous as fungi go. There are only about three to four thousand species of them but in economic significance and in biologic complexity they overshadow some of the more numerous kinds.

First, all rusts are obligate parasites; they will grow only in the living tissue of living plants. Second, most of them produce several different kinds of spores, in regular and almost unalterable succession. There are thousands of different fungi that regularly produce two kinds of spores, one mostly during the growing season that facilitates rapid spread and increase and the second during the fall that serves to overwinter and start the fungus off again in the spring. The technical name for this production of different kinds of spores is pleomorphism, which means many forms or different forms."[4] Looked at from the perspective of the survival of the fittest, this particular ~~genera~~ genus has built in several hot back-up systems. If a variation of the fungus fails for some reason,

3   Ibid., pp. 74–76
4   Ibid., p. 106

the back up is in place to perpetuate its survival. By comparison, we humans are extremely exposed to catastrophic risk. Think the plague or the avian flu scare.

Laboulbenailes give us another fascinating story. These fungi are of no apparent importance beyond their remarkable specialization and manner in which they live. "These particular fungi parasitize insects, particularly beetles and can be found throughout the world. They are even found on water beetles. There is nothing particularly unusual about them, but one species can be found only on a specific, single joint of the left hind leg of a given beetle. It does not invade other joints, attack the mouth whiskers, or it wing covers, thorax or chin. It is restricted to this one odd spot on a single type of beetle. This is specialization with a vengeance."[5]

Fungi that attack humans are numerous, diverse, and relatively unknown to the lay community. The first documented fungus disease affecting humans was published in 1880. The field of medical mycology is embryonic. One fungus, the *Actinomyceoses*, closely resembles bacteria and reproduces bi-directionally. It reproduces as would bacteria and at the same time as mycelium. This is another excellent example of having robust defensive and offensive systems to improve survival prospects and reproductive success.

Perhaps the most widely known dangerous fungus is *ergot*. The ergot fungus is the byproduct of poorly handled rye grain. If rye grain is stored improperly, or stored for too long, the ergot will infect the grain. If the tainted fungus is eaten it manifests itself in a number of ways, from mild to extreme hallucinations and visions, to burning sensations in the extremities, to rapid, insidious, and sometimes fatal gangrenous growth. In the extreme

---

5   Ibid., p. 161

cases, if the infected limb is not amputated, the infection will spread and kill its host. Although the source of the malady was unknown for centuries, the effects of ergotism have been chronicled dating as far back as the tenth century. In a remarkably esoteric compilation, *The Phantom Limb Phenomenon*, Douglas Price, M.D., and Neil Twombly, S.J., Ph.D., translated accounts of not just ergotism, but the phenomenon of perceiving a phantom limb. Phantom limb phenomenon (PLP) has been studied extensively, generally following the path of war and the resultant injuries to troops. What has not been given any study are the examples of the folklore motif of loss and restoration of body parts (L&RM). In their compilation of accounts spanning six centuries, there are recurring examples of similar tales. An individual succumbs to "Saint Anthony's Fire," presumably due to ergotism stemming from bad rye. An arm, foot, or leg is amputated to save its victim from excruciating pain and certain death. Then, the most peculiar happened. With sufficient prayer, some of those afflicted with ergotism and the loss of a limb saw the limb regenerate and the victim returned to normal. This seems to make no sense. Mammals are not tadpoles, lizards, or plants. We are however, participants in evolution and carry deeply recessive genes. We are just beginning to understand the structure of DNA and have a superficial understanding of its operating system. Considering that we haven't even figured out how to regrow lost hair, these accounts simply get dismissed as myth, folklore, or inspiring religious hyperbole. But then again, we know very little about fungi.

Many consider the psychoactive members of the fungus kingdom to be sui generis, that is, unique to themselves as a species. There are relatively few members in this group and their molecular structures are complex.

There is also an open question as to how psychoactive fungi operate on the human brain. One theory suggests that the chemical agent inherent in the mushroom produces a change in consciousness. That is to say, the mushroom is viewed as a chemical catalyst. A contravening theory postulates that the altered consciousness already exists and is simply released by the chemical agent delivered by the mushroom. This theory is much more complex and philosophically related to quantum physics. Quantum physics theorizes that all conditions or potential outcomes exist in varying numbers of parallel universes. The theory includes, among its tenets, that any combination of atoms eventually repeats itself. A human is a combination of atoms, as is the context in which that human exists.

Regardless of the biochemical mechanics or the nature of the universe, the effects of psychotropics express themselves. If, however, the altered consciousness is in fact dormant and waiting for a trigger, larger questions about inter-species sympathetic reactions, particularly within the context of wide scale mimetic impacts, become important areas of thought.

Many, many questions surround the ubiquitous mushroom or fungus. We could not survive without them and beyond the obvious ones, they are generally unknown to most people. Mushroom spores, being very lightweight, travel extremely easily and quickly, invisibly landing on suitable host sites such as rotting wood, field or forest litter, other organic material, or other hosts. Spores are easily dispersed by the wind and can survive extreme ranges of temperature, particularly the cold. They have a long fecundity curve and are classified as super survivors.

There has been speculation for decades by mycologists that some forms of mushrooms or other fungi have drifted through our solar system or beyond, for millennia. Some further speculate that millions of years ago, they landed on earth's biologically hospitable and fertile environment. Coincidentally, this theory is compatible with the speculations and theories of Crick who believed that the spark for life on earth was not just a primordial soup, but rather one stirred up by an unmanned spaceship carrying the seeds of life. Crick may have been correct, but rather than a spaceship, the travelers may have been spores drifting through the vastness of space with the evolutionary objective being to land on fertile territory and reproduce. Late in his life, Crick in fact speculated about a spore-producing planet. These spores, being more or less impervious to extreme cold and morphologically similar to the Homo sapiens, did find a hospitable environment when they landed on the young earth hundreds of millions of years ago. Once the ball got rolling, evolution took its course. Unlike the mushroom cap, which dies off and disappears quickly, the mycelium lives off its host for many years, annually producing fruit for the mushroom cap and stem. This is why mushroom hunters—those collecting morels for example—keep their knowledge secret. They know with reasonable precision where and when the edible form of the mushroom will present itself. Picking a mushroom is similar to picking fruit such as a pear or an apple from a tree. The tree lives on and its yearly bounty of fruit is produced. This is also the case with the mushroom's mycelium. The mycelia remain behind to produce new fruit each year. The difference between the fruit tree and the mycelia is that the latter remains subterranean and invisible whereas the fruit tree stands tall and is a constant reminder to all that its bounty is available to even to those with the least discerning eye. The fungus, on the other hand, is reserved for only those with the curiosity, intellectual capacity, and memory to ferret them out. There is a built-in natural selection in the consumption of many types of mushrooms, particularly those with psychotropic properties. They appear to be reserved for those close to the right side of the intellectual bell curve; that is to say, the smarter of the modern humans.

The Missing Ingredient

Along with major advances in pharmacology, medicine, and psychotherapy, there was the most widespread change in social consciousness and cultural awakening since the Renaissance. Richard Dawkins, in his groundbreaking book, *The Selfish Gene*, theorized that pieces of thought, individual or shared experiences, behave in the same manner as genes. That is, they, the thoughts, tend to replicate themselves in the interest of self-preservation. The ideas tend to seek out and find like-minded hosts and replicate. He defined and named them memes. If there ever was a good example of a memish moment or meme-centric period, it was during the 1960s social revolution in the United States.

Cultural or widespread social change can occur whenever a captivating and contagious thought or cause enters the public theater. Many still have vivid images of longhaired, colorfully clothed youth dancing in the parks of San Francisco in the 1960s. The flower children were perhaps the greatest manifestation of the meme concept in the world's recent history. This contagion of enlightenment changed legislation, elected fresh blood into political positions and contributed in no small way to ending the unpopular war in Vietnam. Considering the book was published in 1976, it is safe to assume this social movement had at least a small role in contributing to Dawkins' theory. Similarly impacted was the field of chemically based recreation. Once can theorize that LSD opened the eyes of many; enough to reach a tipping point. People did turn on, tune in, and drop out. Things changed.

Today, we live in a troubled world. A world with crippling financial debt, a world with extreme political and religious polarization, a world with too many wars and too many people. We have laws that make no sense, widespread corruption, deteriorating educational systems, and obsolete infrastructure. Making all of this seem far worse than it is—and it is a very bad state of affairs—there is too much apathy.

Where is the outrage today?

Further Reading

Crick, Francis, (1982). Life Itself: Its Origin and Nature. Touchstone, Simon & Schuster.

Urey, Harold, (1952). The Planets: Their Origin and Development. Yale University Press.

Dawkins, Richard, (1976). The Selfish Gene. Oxford University Press.

Forethought

Aspects of the manuscript have benefited by conversations with M. O. Dillon, J. Guenther, K. Bonello, R. Harris, R. Krinker, P.P. Bonello, P.J. Bonello, J.Dorris, V. Wright, M. Whelen and many others. Thanks to also to Wikipedia.

A special note of thanks and appreciation to Victoria Wright for her thoughtful editing, keen insights and delightful personality.

Endnotes

1 Phantastic, Louis Lewin, Wikipedia
2 The Botany and Chemistry of Hallucinogenic Plants, Shultes and Hoffman, 1979, pg, 15.
3 The Botany of Desire, Michael Pollan, pg, 143, Random House Publishing, 2001
4 Raoul Mourgue, Am J Psychiatry 89:1364-1366, May 1933
5 James South, 5-HTP (5-Hydroxytryptophan): The Serotonin Solution, 2nd September 2004.
6 Nothing's Going to Change My World, Lennon-McCartney, "Across the Universe" was first released in this version on the Regal Starline SRS 5013 album, No One's Gonna Change Our World, December, 1969
   Notes on song's history, Wikipedia, September 20, 9:20 CST.

February 1968 recordings

In February 1968, the Beatles convened at the EMI Abbey Road studios to record a single for release during their absence on their forthcoming trip to India. Paul McCartney had written "Lady Madonna" and Lennon, "Across the Universe". Both tracks were recorded along with Lennon's "Hey Bulldog" and the vocal track for George's "The Inner Light" between the 3 and 11 of February.

The basic track was successfully recorded on 4 February. Along with the basic rhythm track of acoustic guitar, percussion and tambura, it featured an overdubbed sitar introduction by George Harrison. Two teenaged fans, Lizzie Bravo and Gayleen Pease, were invited in off the street to provide backup vocals.

Lennon still wasn't satisfied with the feel of the track and several sound effects were taped, including 15 seconds of humming and a guitar and a harp-like sound, both to be played backwards; however, none of these were used on the released version. The track was mixed to mono and put aside as the group had decided to release "Lady Madonna" and "The Inner Light" as the single. On their return from India, the group set about recording the many songs they had written there, and "Across the Universe" remained on the shelf. In the autumn of 1968, the Beatles seriously considered releasing an EP including most of the songs for the *Yellow Submarine* album and "Across the Universe", and went as far as having the EP mastered.

World Wildlife Fund version

During the February 1968 recording sessions, Spike Milligan dropped into the studio and, on hearing the song, suggested the track would be ideal for release on a charity album he was organising for the World Wildlife Fund. At some point in 1968, the Beatles agreed to this proposal. In January 1969, the best mono mix was remixed for the charity album[8]. In keeping with the "wildlife" theme of the album, sound effects of birds were added to the beginning and end. The original (mono) mix from February 1968 is 3:37 minutes in length. After the effects were added, the track was sped up so that even with 20 seconds of effects, it is only 3:49. By October 1969, it was decided that the song needed to be remixed into stereo. This was done by Geoff Emerick immediately prior to the banding of the album. "Across the Universe" was first released in this version on the Regal Starline SRS 5013 album, *No One's Gonna Change Our World*, in December 1969.

This version was issued on three Beatle compilation albums, the British version of *Rarities*, the different American version of *Rarities* and the second disc of the two-CD *Past Masters* album.

Let It Be version

The Beatles took the song up again during the *Get Back/Let It Be* rehearsal sessions of January 1969; footage of Lennon playing the song appeared in the *Let It Be* movie. Bootleg recordings from the sessions include numerous full group performances of the song, usually with Lennon–McCartney harmonies on the chorus. To ensure the album tied in with the film it was decided the song must be included on what by January 1970 had become the *Let It Be* album. Also, Lennon's contributions to the sessions were sparse, and this unreleased piece was seen as a way to fill the gap.

Although the song was extensively rehearsed on the

Twickenham Studios soundstage the only recordings were mono transcriptions for use in the film soundtrack. No multitrack recordings were made after the group's move to Apple Studios. Thus in early January 1970 Glyn Johns remixed the February 1968 recording. The new mix omitted the teenaged girls' vocals and the bird sound effects of the World Wildlife Fund version. As neither of the Glyn Johns *Get Back* albums were officially released, the version most people are familiar with came from Phil Spector, who in late March and early April 1970 remixed the February 1968 recording yet again and added orchestral and choral overdubs. Spector also slowed the track to 3:47, close to its original speed. According to Lennon, "Spector took the tape and did a damn good job with it."

Plaudite, amici, comoedia finita est.